"Maybe ...... ther a little b.....

"But I was ....g that you didn't wa..... know me better, so I thought I'd speed things up a little bit." Devon grinned his signature, megawatt, killer grin. The one that used to inspire girls to throw their panties at him up on stage.

Kylie shook her head at him.

"What?"

"You," she pronounced, "are a mess."

"You think I don't know that?"

Then she nodded, drumming her fingers on her champagne glass. "I think you might do."

"Do?"

"Mmm-hmm. You just might." But then she turned on her heel and walked away, her actions, like her words, sending damned confusing signals.

Devon downed the rest of the hated champagne. Then in three long strides he caught up to Kylie and stepped in front of her. "I'll *do?* Do *what,* exactly?"

She flashed that Swiss-bank-vault smile. Then she patted his cheek. Her touch sent an electric current through him, from his jaw to his toes and then back up to toast everything south of the border.

"Me," she replied. Then she walked off again, leaving him staring in her wake.

Dear Reader,

There are so many reality TV shows that feature ex-rockers, superstars whose posters we may have had on our bedroom walls when we were twelve. This made me wonder what life becomes for a guy who once took the spotlight for granted, yet now is just a regular Joe. It's got to be a tough adjustment, no?

And so former bad boy Devon McKee and his black leather pants were born. He's the second groomsman in my All the Groom's Men trilogy.

Dev's got a big heart and a lot of emotional baggage, but likes to pretend that he doesn't. A serial womanizer, he now wants a *real* relationship with a woman, but he's not quite sure how to go about it—even though he's spotted the right woman in Kylie Kent.

But Kylie's got his number—and refuses to give him hers. The very last thing she wants is another degenerate man in her life. She just got rid of one, thank you very much. Her career and a cat will do fine....

I hope you enjoy Dev's story as much as I enjoyed writing it! Let me know by contacting me through my website, www.KarenKendall.com.

Happy reading,

Karen Kendall

Karen Kendall

BLAME IT ON THE BACHELOR

TORONTO NEW YORK LONDON
AMSTERDAM PARIS SYDNEY HAMBURG
STOCKHOLM ATHENS TOKYO MILAN MADRID
PRAGUE WARSAW BUDAPEST AUCKLAND

Recycling programs
for this product may
not exist in your area.

ISBN-13: 978-0-373-79677-9

BLAME IT ON THE BACHELOR

This edition published by arrangement with Harlequin Books S.A.

For questions and comments about the quality of this book please contact us at Customer_eCare@Harlequin.ca.

® and TM are trademarks of the publisher. Trademarks indicated with ® are registered in the United States Patent and Trademark Office, the Canadian Trade Marks Office and in other countries.

www.Harlequin.com

Printed in U.S.A.

ABOUT THE AUTHOR

Karen Kendall is an award-winning, bestselling author of more than twenty novels and novellas, many of them romantic comedies. She is the recipient of a Maggie Award, plus Bookseller's Best, Write Touch and *RT Book Reviews* Reviewers' Choice Awards. Karen lives and laughs in south Florida with her husband, two rescue greyhounds and one cat. She loves hearing from readers! Please visit her website at www.KarenKendall.com.

Books by Karen Kendall

To get the inside scoop on Harlequin Blaze and its talented writers, be sure to check out blazeauthors.com.

All backlist available in ebook. Don't miss any of our special offers. Write to us at the following address for information on our newest releases.

Harlequin Reader Service
U.S.: 3010 Walden Ave., P.O. Box 1325, Buffalo, NY 14269
Canadian: P.O. Box 609, Fort Erie, Ont. L2A 5X3

For Don, who has always been my rock star.

Acknowledgments

With special thanks to my consultants on all things Swedish; Julita Zaborovsky and Martin Pirgiotis. Chef Bodvar wouldn't be the same without you!

1

DEVON MCKEE FELT LIKE a hyena at high tea. He did *not* belong at a fussy rehearsal dinner in a country club. But he was a groomsman, and the wedding party and all the relatives had been invited, so here he was. Chatting with his buddy's Great Aunt Mildred and trying to resist the urge to add about four ounces of rum to his plain Coke.

If he added the rum, he'd be all too responsible for the consequences. He might do things that he'd regret—and his head still ached from the bachelor party the previous night.

Mark was getting married, and for Mark's sake, Dev would do his best impression of a gentleman, comical though the act might be.

He'd known Mark since college and he loved him like a brother. He might heckle him about going over to the Dark Side, but he was secretly envious—and that was just plain weird.

Dev first spied the girl of his dreams through Aunt Mildred's hairdo, which was teased and sprayed to an awe-inspiring volume, in spite of its sparseness. Aunt Mildred's hair—a spiderweb combed into an upside-down urn shape—was almost transparent, gossamer in the overhead lighting.

Through it, Dev got a glimpse of the girl. She had a smile

like a Swiss bank account: secure, glamorous and a bit secretive. A regal neck and aristocratic shoulders, revealed to perfection in her short, navy silk dress. Dark blond hair with shimmers of gold throughout. And legs that were nothing short of spectacular.

Devon, once the lead guitarist for the Miami band Category Five, was a connoisseur of such things. He'd always been a leg man—not that he disliked cleavage or sassy asses. Far from it. And he saw plenty of those now that he'd opened a successful South Beach bar.

What he didn't always see was—no other word for it—class. This woman dripped it the same way many others oozed availability. She fit in perfectly here in the country club's garden room.

His first coherent thought was that he wanted to lick those incredible legs of hers—but *not* through Aunt Mildred's hairdo. So he extricated his hand from the old lady's and told her he'd return with a glass of champagne for her.

Dev swam, sharklike, through the crowd and up to the bar, where he secured two champagnes before he continued toward the delicious woman, his dorsal fin flying high. In no time at all, he was in front of her. He opened his mouth, sure that one of his famous one-liners would emerge and make her giggle.

But nothing happened. His mojo, his schmooze, his charm—they'd deserted him. He searched blindly for a word, any word, even a grunt. But he'd been struck dumb.

Finally, Dev closed his mouth.

She lifted an elegant eyebrow, clearly amused at his expense.

Embarrassed and trying to recover, he dropped his gaze to her breasts. She had very nice ones. C cup, he estimated. Friendly, they seemed to surge toward him, eager to make his acquaintance.

"Hi," Dev said to them. "Uh. Mark thought you might like some champagne." A lame line, but workable.

Naturally enough, the breasts did not respond. Instead, their owner did. "Mark's not even here yet." Her voice was rich, smooth, spicy like the Jamaican rum he craved.

He blinked at her, feeling like an idiot. Mark *hadn't* arrived yet.

"But the twins never turn down tiny bubbles." She smiled at him and neatly plucked both glasses from his fingers, holding them in front of her breasts. Then she raised one to her lips. "So thanks."

From somewhere over his shoulder, Dev heard a hoot of male laughter that could only have come from Pete Dale, another groomsman. Pete *would* have to witness Dev's humiliation. But he'd deal with him later.

Dev slowly raised his eyes to the woman's, heat suffusing his face. This was the worst encounter he'd had with a girl since ninth grade. "I…um. I guess I deserved that."

Her smile dissolved into laughter and she handed him back the other champagne glass. "Admit it. Mark had nothing to do with you coming over here."

Devon hated champagne—it tasted like sour tonic water to him—but he upended the flute and drank half the contents in one gulp. "Okay," he said. "I do admit it. What's your name?"

"I'm Kylie Kent. You?"

"Devon McKee."

"Devon," she repeated, thoughtfully.

"How do you know Mark?" he asked.

"I'm his aunt."

"His *what?*"

"His aunt. Even though he's older than I am. It's kind of weird, but true."

Dev digested that, working out the math. He guessed it was

possible that Mark's father or mother had a much younger sister.

Kylie was doing some thinking of her own. "Wait… Devon…you're Mark's rock-star friend?"

"I was never more than a minor local celebrity."

"Mark mentioned you. And I guess that explains the leather pants."

"Er." He'd never before felt the need to explain those, but now, in her presence, he wished he'd worn something boring and khaki. He wished he'd tamped down his spiked, rocker hair and maybe even left his gold chain at home. He was crashing and burning here, big-time.

"Not that they're not very nice leather pants," she added, evaluating them.

"Yeah, okay. You hate my pants. Whatever." He raised his chin and angled his head down at her. If she weren't so damned hot, he'd be cutting his losses and walking away right now. Dev, heretofore the coolest guy in Miami, felt like the city's biggest dork. It wasn't a feeling he liked.

"I don't hate them at all," Kylie said. "I want them myself."

"No kidding?" Dev asked. "Here, you can have 'em right now." Tongue between his teeth, he went for his fly. After all, he had to recover his man card *somehow*.

She laughed. "Maybe we should get to know each other a little better first."

"You think?"

"Yes." She tilted her champagne glass towards her perfect lips and drank.

"Well, but I was getting the distinct feeling that you didn't *want* to get to know me better, so I thought I'd speed things up a little bit." He grinned his signature, megawatt, killer grin. The one that used to inspire girls to throw their panties at him up on stage.

She shook her head at him.

"What?" He waggled his eyebrows at her.

"You," she pronounced, "are a mess."

"You think I don't know that?"

She pursed her perfect lips. "But you have a peculiar, repulsive appeal," she said thoughtfully.

Dev blinked. He wasn't sure he liked the sound of that.

She nodded, drumming her fingers on her glass. "I think you might do."

"Do?"

"Mmm, hmm. You just might." But then she turned on her heel and walked away, her actions, like her words, sending damned confusing signals.

How could a guy be repellent and have appeal at the same time? It didn't make any sense.

Devon upended his glass again and sucked down the rest of the hated champagne. Then in three long strides he caught up to Kylie and stepped in front of her. "I'll *do?* Do *what,* exactly?"

She flashed that Swiss-bank-vault smile again. Then she patted his cheek. Her touch sent an electric current through him, from his jaw to his toes and then up to toast his balls.

"Me," she replied. Then she walked off again, leaving him staring in her wake.

KYLIE FORCED HERSELF to keep her shoulders straight and didn't permit herself to turn around as she walked to the ladies' room. She was pretty sure that Mr. Black Leather Pants was still standing there with his mouth hanging open, and she relished the moment.

Kylie, girl, you've still got it. Or you can at least fake it. See?

Nobody needed to know that she was a loser who couldn't keep her own fiancé's interest. Nobody needed to know that she'd lost him to internet porn.

Kylie entered the fussy, overdecorated ladies' lounge and stepped up to the wide gilt mirror, where she took a quick inventory of her face. Eyeliner: currently unsmudged. Blusher: fine. Nose: a smidgeon shiny.

She reached into her bag for her compact, pleased to note that her hands were steady. She powdered her nose, adding a layer to what she thought of as her "war paint" for the evening.

She studied her reflection critically. Everything was more or less symmetrical. She had nice hazel eyes. She was no dog. So why had Jack felt the need to—

Who knew. Why had Tiger Woods cheated on his absolutely stunning wife?

Well, sweetie…men do like variety, you know. Maybe some racy lingerie, a wig or a little role-playing would help.

Kylie jammed the compact into her purse with a little more force than necessary as she remembered her older sister's well-meaning hints. *Note to self: never complain about your sex life to your relatives!*

Not only was her sister's advice annoying and humiliating, but it also conjured up all kinds of horrible specters about what she might have gotten up to over the years.

Kylie shuddered and pulled out a lipstick. There was nothing to touch up, but she did anyway, killing time before she had to return to the garden room. Small talk wasn't her favorite thing.

At least it's only internet pictures, her sister had said. *Yeah, sis. Right. A lot you know.*

It would have been better, really, if Jack had cheated on her with a real woman—or even two. Imperfect women with stressful jobs and ungrateful children and PMS.

But she simply couldn't compete with a constant parade of flawless, airbrushed beauties and their bountiful beaver shots.

Jack could pull them up at any time for his viewing pleasure. And he did.

How pathetic he was, sitting in the dark with his porn. So why did *she* feel like the loser? She was crazy.

Kylie had finally had enough of the repeated talks and the repeated broken promises to stop. She'd dumped his sorry ass.

If only she didn't remember what Jack was like before he'd discovered OxyContin and internet porn. He'd been handsome and charming, with a bright future in medical equipment sales ahead of him.

He'd been a blue-blazer kind of guy, definitely not the type to show up to a coat-and-tie dinner in, say, black leather pants.

But Jack was now unemployed and boozing it up in T-shirts that said things like I'm with Stupid, and Property of So-and-So's Athletic Department. He needed a barber badly and a life even more.

And it was time for Kylie to focus on what she herself needed: to wash Jack out of her hair for good.

She needed a distraction.

A male distraction, one with no conscience so she wouldn't feel at all bad about using him for her own psychological and physical purposes.

Yes, she needed some acrobatic, sweaty, therapeutic sex with a hot stranger. A stranger who wouldn't want a relationship, since she was done with those for a while. A stranger who was ready to peel off his inappropriate pants within moments of finding out her name.

Devon McKee had honed right in on her. Devon, with his I'm-a-sex-god eyes and his background full of rock 'n' roll groupies, was just the ticket. Her ticket to ride.

He'd do quite handsomely.

And she was sure he'd do her well.

2

Devon, after a moment of stunned silence, followed Kylie out of the reception, only to see her disappear behind the door of the ladies' room.

There was no question that given the opportunity he would *do* her. But he didn't like the way she'd neatly plucked the power out of his hands along with the champagne glasses. He felt like a piece of meat.

He had a mental image of Kylie poking and prodding him through plastic wrap as he sat on a foam tray in the cold case of the local supermarket.

Repulsive appeal?

As if he had an area of gristle or a streak of fat running through him, and she wasn't sure he was worth his per-pound price. As if she'd take him home in a pinch, but was tempted to wait until he oxidized a little and went on sale.

That stuck in his craw.

Devon McKee of Category Five had been Grade A prime beef in his heyday. Hell, he'd had a local artist make a mobile of the lacy thongs that had been tossed at him. He'd had the bad taste to hang it over his pool table in the game room of his rented house.

He wasn't particularly proud of that now, but then, he wasn't proud of a lot of things he'd done.

Kylie Kent was right. He *was* a mess. But he wasn't used to being summed up so thoroughly and instantaneously by a woman. And he'd already decided to start cleaning himself up. Maybe not today. But soon.

"Dev, what are you doing lurking out here in the hallway?" Adam asked him. Adam Chase, a medical student, was the best man, and he was currently sporting a broken nose. Or close to broken, anyway.

"Nice schnoz. Where's the stripper you stole from the bachelor party last night? You didn't bring her as a date?"

Adam glowered at him, and Dev grinned.

The very cute blond stripper had exploded out of her plywood cake only to elbow his friend right in the face, knocking him to the floor.

Adam squinted at the champagne flute Dev held and deliberately changed the subject. "What's with that? You hate champagne."

"Yeah, but I'm trying to stay away from the rum."

"Since when?"

Dev waved a hand at him and ambled into the garden room. He went to the bar and then belatedly brought Aunt Mildred the drink he'd promised her.

She arched a drawn-on eyebrow at him. "Thank you, young man. Did you have to harvest the grapes, first?"

Was every woman here, from five to ninety, going to bust his balls? But his lips twitched. "Yes, ma'am. Apologies."

She patted his arm. "It's all right. I saw you almost trip over your tongue when Kylie walked in. The girl's always been a looker. Sweet, too."

Sweet?

"She's far too wholesome for you, dear. Wait until tomorrow at the wedding and I'll introduce you to a naughty girl who's more your speed." Aunt Mildred, to his horror, winked at him.

For the second time in a half hour, Dev found himself speechless. Then he got defensive. "How do you know I'm not looking for a nice girl?"

She cackled. "In those pants?"

Damn it, he was going to set fire to them.

"I really am looking to settle down. You know, find the One. Believe it or not." He wasn't sure he believed it himself, but the words had somehow flown out of his mouth.

Mildred eyed him shrewdly. "Your tone is sincere. But are you serious or…self-delusional?"

Dev laughed weakly because he had no idea how to respond.

Was he self-delusional? After all, he'd just failed the challenge his sister Ciara had set him: to keep a houseplant and a goldfish alive for a month. She'd gotten the idea from some movie.

Anyway, the plant had died after ten days, despite his best efforts. And the fish was looking depressed and moody. He hoped the neighbor kid wasn't overfeeding it while he was away for the weekend. Or forgetting to feed it at all.

"Why are you abusing me, Aunt Mildred?" Dev asked her, with his best innocent-little-boy smile.

"I'm not, dear heart. I'm fond of you, and I don't want to see you make a mistake. My first husband thought he was ready to settle down with a nice girl, too." She lifted her shoulders and took a sip of her champagne, leaving a mauve lipprint on the rim of the glass. "He wasn't."

"I'm sorry."

"Don't be. If Laurence hadn't done me wrong, I'd never have met Mr. Right. Ed and I were married for forty-three years, all of them good. But I won't lie to you—it's easier to get it straight the first time." She smiled at him. "So you make sure that you sow every last one of your wild oats before you go playing house, hmmm?"

Just what, exactly, *was* a wild oat? *Wild* and *oats* had never seemed to fit together, to Dev. And *sow* meant to plant. If something was planted, then it didn't grow wild. Where did these phrases come from?

But all he said was, "Yes, ma'am. Thank you for the advice. Now, can I get you a shrimp puff or a Swedish meatball?"

"No, Devon, but thank you. Run along now and play with someone your own age." She tilted her cheek up and he dutifully kissed it.

As he moved away, he caught Pete smirking good-naturedly at him. "What?" he growled.

"That blonde you hit on a few minutes ago?" Pete chuckled. "I've never seen the mighty McKee shut down so hard."

"Oh, yeah? It might interest you to know that she wants to do me."

His buddy guffawed. "Oh, clearly. I suppose she told you that right up front."

"As a matter of fact, she did. So you can save your sarcasm." Dev swiped a shrimp puff off a passing waiter's tray and popped it into his mouth.

"You lie," Pete said. "Like a rug."

Pete could say things like that to him, because they'd known each other for over a decade—since freshman year in college. All the groomsmen had. They'd all been pledges in the same fraternity.

Dev didn't respond, because Kylie Kent chose that moment to undulate through the doorway and wink at him.

Women didn't wink at him. He winked at them. How dare she seize the power of the wink *and* the one-liner? Things were all out of whack, here. Off-kilter. Askew.

He was the wolf. She was Little Red Riding Hood. They needed to get the rules straight, here.

Dev shoved his hands into his pockets and sauntered toward her with a scowl on his face. She'd plucked another glass of champagne off a waiter's tray and moved into a corner.

Just as she held it to her lips to take a sip, he reached her and leaned into her space. "Where do you get off?" he asked indignantly.

She raised her eyes to his, amusement in them. "Where? Or how? Use your imagination. I have the same parts as other women."

Again, she'd rendered him speechless. Wholesome? Had Aunt Mildred really called her *wholesome,* for God's sake?

"But if you want to know where…" She shrugged. "There's a utility closet down the hall from the ladies' room. You can't miss it."

Devon found his voice. "You know damned well what I mean. You've got a hell of a nerve, Kylie Kent. What makes you so sure I'd do you?"

She tilted her head at him. "You undressed me with your eyes as soon as I walked into the room."

"So?" Dev said, flushing in spite of himself. "It's a disgusting male habit I have. It doesn't make you special."

"Then you brought me a drink."

"A more polite male habit."

"And you talked to my breasts."

"So you have a nice rack."

"McKee," she said patiently, "just admit it. You want to have sex with me."

"Yeah?" said Dev, outraged. "Honey, I've got news for you. I wouldn't bang you if you were the last chick on earth."

"That's your pride talking, not your dick."

His mouth fell open. How dare she? "You are *so* full of it."

"Is that right?" she smiled. She dropped her gaze to his

fly, which made him uncomfortable. *Him,* of all people. She drank deeply from her glass.

Then she wet her lips and peered up at him from under her lashes. "I'll bet it's big," she whispered. "Isn't it?"

The breath he was taking turned to a rasp in his throat.

"And I'm so ready for it. Did you know I'm not wearing any panties? What do you think about that, Dev?"

The air he'd drawn in refused to circulate. It stayed there and rattled helplessly in his windpipe.

"I'll bet you like sex fast and hard…with her ankles on your shoulders…unless her mouth is on you, taking it all the way in…."

And just like that, Devon was wearing an erection as well as a tie to Mark's rehearsal dinner.

He was furious, and yet he was filled with an unwilling admiration for her as well as lust. She had definitely called his bluff. "You're a world-class witch," he said to Kylie.

"I'm really not." Was there a hint of apology in her tone?

He let out a bark of laughter as he buttoned his jacket and held his glass strategically in front of himself.

"I was only trying to make—" She broke off, looking—of all things—abashed.

He didn't buy the act for a second. "Make what, darlin'?" he asked sardonically.

She hesitated. "A point."

That hadn't been what she was going to say. He knew it instinctively. "Well, you did." He looked down at his crotch. "You made your point and now I'm stuck with it," he said bitterly. "Thanks."

"I'll help you with that," she said, evidently emboldened again. "Really. Just meet me in the utility closet in five."

He gritted his teeth and leaned forward so that his lips almost brushed her ear. He could smell her honeysuckle shampoo, her light floral perfume, the clean scent of her skin. "Not even if the fate of the free world depended on it."

Kylie gulped the last of her champagne. Was it his imagination, or was her lip trembling?

He didn't care. "But you go ahead to that closet. You just hop on your broomstick and enjoy yourself, sweetheart. You hear?"

With that parting shot, Dev turned on his heel and walked away without compunction—still horny as all get-out.

Damn her.

3

KYLIE WAS SHAKING INSIDE, though she wore her smile like armor. What was wrong with her, that she couldn't even score with a bona fide man-whore like Devon McKee? His reputation preceded him. Everyone knew he had no standards; that given the chance he'd do a day-old bagel.

And yet he'd turned her down, despite the fact that she'd lost her mind and talked to him like a professional phone-sex operator.

The cocktail hour was drawing to a close and soon everyone would take their assigned seats for dinner. She was on the verge of tears. She had to pull herself together.

Kylie lifted yet another glass of champagne—her third—from a waiter's tray and wobbled towards the ladies' room again, with the idea of shutting herself into a stall until she'd calmed down. But the entire flock of bridesmaids got there before she did, leaving her no option…except, perhaps, the infamous utility closet.

A quick scan of the hallway told her she was alone, so she walked quickly to the door, pulled it open and slipped inside, feeling around for a light switch as she closed herself in.

Far from being alone with a sexy ex-rocker, she had as her companions an industrial carpet steamer, a cart stocked with cleaning products and bathroom tissue, and a vacuum the size of a Chevrolet.

Kylie leaned her forehead against one of the dingy, pock-marked walls and closed her eyes against the sting of rejection. It wasn't really Devon's rejection that hurt, of course—it was the long months of feeling inadequate in her relationship, helpless at the erosion of Jack's love as drugs and sexual fantasy consumed him.

Devon's dismissal of her was the last straw. Kylie gulped the entire glass of champagne and set the flute on the cleaning cart. She took a deep breath. Then another.

I will not cry. I will absolutely not cry. I will under no circumstances cry.

I am a strong, fabulous woman with a great job in banking. I will be an assistant vice president soon, then a regional vice president of the bank one day. If I can't have a fulfilling personal life, then I will have a meteoric career.

There is no reason for me to be skulking in a broom closet! I will not cry...

Oh, hell. Did salt water stain silk? She was going to ruin her dress. Kylie grabbed a roll of toilet paper from the cleaning cart and unwound enough to mummify her entire head. She buried her face in it.

Judging by the black streaks on the tissue, her mascara was running, damn it. She had to stop this pathetic mewling immediately.

Bank executives did not behave this way.

She straightened her spine and looked upward, blinking rapidly to get rid of the tears in her eyes. She smacked her own cheeks lightly. She cleared her throat.

"I am woman," Kylie said out loud. "Hear me roar."

Of course that was the moment when the closet door opened, and Devon McKee stood staring down at her, his dark eyebrows raised quizzically.

"Roar?" he asked.

Really, why couldn't the floor swallow her up?

"I heard some sniffling," he said, "but definitely no roaring."

"Figure of speech." She tried to brush past him—but he didn't move.

Instead, he closed the door behind them, forcing her to step back. "What's the matter, darlin'?"

"Nothing. I—I need to go find my seat. They'll start serving dinner any minute, now."

"Word of advice?"

"What?" she asked gruffly.

"Clean up your face a little better. It looks like a kid's finger painting. Here, let me help." He cupped her face in his hands and rubbed gently under her eyes with his thumbs. He brushed at her cheeks with his fingers. And then he dabbed at her mouth with a piece of the bathroom tissue.

Mortifying though the situation was, the warmth—and was it tenderness?—of his hands sent shivers of renegade pleasure down her spine and brought heat to the surface of her face and neck.

"That's better," Devon said. "Not that you weren't the most gorgeous human finger painting alive."

She managed a self-deprecating snuffle.

"Now, do you want to tell ol' Dev why you're crying in this closet?"

"Not crying," she muttered.

"*Riiiight.* So, do you want to tell me why you're squeezing joy and happiness out of your eyes in secret, then?"

She shook her head.

"I see. Well, I just want to make sure that all this, um, *euphoria* isn't because of something that a nasty pecker-head said to you a few minutes ago in defense of his own ego."

"Of course not," she said emphatically.

"I'm so relieved. I mean, this really sets my mind at ease," said Devon, frowning at her.

"Good."

He looked around the closet. "It's clear to me, in that case, that you came in here to have fun with your broomstick, as the nasty pecker-head suggested."

Kylie's lips quivered in spite of her mood.

"But it's gone," he pointed out. "So…"

She met his eyes, which were twinkling ruefully. "The carpet steamer was more than adequate."

"Ah. Need a cigarette now, do you?"

She nodded.

He patted his pockets.

"Actually, I don't smoke."

They stood looking at each other for a long moment, and she had to admit that if any guy could carry off leather pants, it most certainly was Devon McKee.

"I'm sorry," she said.

"I'm sorry," he said simultaneously.

They both laughed.

"I'm not normally a slut or a tease," Kylie added.

"That's a real shame. What was it about me that brought out those admirable, delightful qualities?"

Her face flash-fried. She didn't answer.

"I don't normally play hard to get," Dev said. "But I'm usually in the driver's seat, so to speak. This was a whole new ball game."

"Yeah…listen, we really should get back out there." Once again, Kylie tried to maneuver her way out of the closet.

Once again, Dev blocked her way, this time, by simply stretching his arms across the narrow breadth of the closet and putting his palms flat on each wall.

Kylie eyed him nervously.

"Not that it wasn't refreshing, but I prefer to do the seducing," he said with a predatory grin.

My, but he had a lot of very white teeth. Rather wolfish ones, truth to tell.

She swallowed nervously, all of her former bravado having deserted her. She was locked in a closet with a guy she didn't really know, and she'd teased him shamelessly.

Dev's arm shot out and he caught her around the back of her neck, under her hair. Her stomach flipped as he drew her inexorably toward him. She was barely aware of her feet moving, or of her knees shaking as he bent his head to hers.

His lips sent liquid fire shooting through her veins, and they parted hers easily. He delved into her mouth, his other hand slipping down her back, over the thin silk of her dress. He pulled her against him, hard, and his hand drifted lower, cupping her bottom and then curving up again.

"You lied," he said. "You *are* wearing panties. A thong."

He slid his fingers up, under her dress, and the heat of him against her bare flesh shocked and excited her.

"So smooth," he murmured. "So soft."

She gasped as he dipped under the thong, into the cleft of her backside and down to the most private area of her body. The pleasure exquisite, it sent erotic ripples all over her body. He released her nape and picked her up with both hands, her skirt rucked up and the core of her snug against the hardness of him.

His breath came hot and shallow against her lips as he rocked against her, doing through their clothing what he wanted to do naked.

Through her dress, her breasts rubbed against his shirt, aching and wanting.

Supporting her weight with his left hand, he went back to cause more sensual trouble with his right. He dipped under her thong again, stroking and rubbing.

The sensations held her at gunpoint, taut and caught on a moan and shivering at the possibility of what he might do next.

Devon bit her lower lip gently and slid two fingers into her, still teasing her core with his thumb.

Unintelligible noises came from her own mouth, and she finally tore away from his. "You can't— We can't— You have to put me down!"

"Why?" asked Devon, and did something even more disturbing and wonderful.

"Because—*aaahhhhh…*"

"I thought you wanted me to do you."

"*Ohhhhhhhhhhh.* No, stop! Wait, don't stop—"

"Am I doing you wrong?"

"*Noooooooooo!*"

"Then what's the problem?" He cleared space on the cleaning cart by knocking a bunch of bath tissue off it, then set her down. He fished in his pocket for his wallet and took out a condom. While she caught her breath, he unzipped his pants and rolled the condom on.

She couldn't help being stunned at the size of him. She also couldn't help coming to her senses about their ugly surroundings. "This is really cheap and sleazy," she said, as he picked her up again.

"I know." He grinned. "Ain't it grand?" And he lowered her slowly onto his cock, kissing her as she reacted with a helpless moan. "You're so tight. So hot. So delicious. Mmm."

"I'm such a *slut!*"

He chuckled, nuzzling her neck. "Yeah, that's right. Feel guilty about it, feel dirty. 'Cause I'm gonna make you come anyway and a filthy, screaming orgasm is the best kind there is. Okay, honey?" He backed her against a wall and gave it to her hard, the way she needed it right now.

She needed passion. She needed to be with someone so excited by her that he could barely control himself. She needed so desperately to be wanted.

Devon supported her now with his right arm and used his left to pin her wrists above her head, driving into her almost violently, taking her to the edge and then beyond. The heat and the friction and the sense of the forbidden built to a crest. Then he bit her nipple lightly through her dress and she lost control, spasming around him.

"That's right, darlin'. That's beautiful. Give it to me, give me all you've got." It was his turn to groan, now, as he took himself to the hilt inside of her, once and twice and a third, final time. He cursed softly as he came and held her to him tightly until every last tremor between them subsided.

Kylie leaned her head against the wall, her eyes unfocused. Devon kissed her neck and finally put her down, not that she could stand on her own two feet at the moment. She slid down in a boneless heap.

Dev leaned on the supply cart, panting. "You are something else, sweetheart."

She nodded. "I'm now officially a tramp."

He frowned at her. "If you feel this conflicted about things, why did you proposition me to begin with?"

"It's complicated," she said, pulling her dress over her thighs. At least she hadn't thought once about Jack. "Why did you come looking for me? I thought you said that you wouldn't bang me if I were the last chick on the planet. Not if the fate of the free world hung in the balance."

Dev shrugged. "Clearly I'm not superhero material."

"I don't know about that." She shot him a sidelong glance.

"We aim to please, here at McKee, Inc." He winked at her.

"Devon, how are we going to go into the rehearsal dinner without everyone knowing what we just did?"

He pursed his lips. "People knowing is a problem for you?"

"Yes! I'm really not this type of girl."

"The riddle again. So it was my animal magnetism that toppled you from your nice-girl pedestal?"

"Absolutely."

"Why am I not buying this? Why do I have a feeling that you had some twisted female agenda of your very own?"

She gave him a look of limpid innocence.

He snorted. "All right. Now, I'm going to sneak out of here and find a pack of cigarettes. My official story is that I went out for a smoke and lost track of the time. You, on the other hand, got a business call. So you go back in still 'talking' to someone on your cell phone and then hang up and apologize to your table. I'll saunter in about five minutes later, looking surprised that the meal has started. Does that work for you?"

She nodded and got to her feet, smoothing her dress. She found her purse and dug out her lipstick and compact, repairing the damage he'd done.

He watched her silently while he readjusted his own clothes and disposed of the condom. "Okay. One final thing, Kylie Kent."

"What's that?"

His dark eyes crinkled at the corners as he gave her a dazzling smile. "Well, I'd like your phone number, of course."

She froze for a moment, then shook her head decisively as the smile dropped off his face. "Oh, no, no, no. No offense— you were great—but I don't think that's a good idea at all."

And Kylie bolted out of the supply closet, once again leaving him speechless.

4

OUTSIDE, DEV SUCKED HARD on his Marlboro Red and squinted at the duck in front of him. It tilted its head and stared at him out of black eyes that would have been menacing on any other creature.

"You want bread. I want a phone number. Life sucks, buddy. That's all I can tell you." Dev blew smoke out of his mouth and nostrils, feeling like a disgruntled animal himself—some sort of hairy, two-legged dragon.

The duck opened its beak and expelled a hiss of displeasure before turning its tail feathers on him and waddling to the edge of a man-made pond.

A couple of smaller ducks bobbed on the surface of the water. Big Duck sailed toward them grumpily, then without notice flapped his wings and climbed onto one of the others, shoving her half under the water. Rustling and squawking ensued. It took Dev a minute to clue in.

"Dude," he said, shaking his head. "That's just wrong." At least *his* woman had been willing. "And you could, at a *minimum,* buy her dinner first."

After the unromantic, er, ducking, the female emerged outraged and shook herself off, clearly wanting nothing further to do with Big Duck.

"Feeling used?" Dev asked. "Me, too." He finished his cigarette and left the butt in the sand on top of a trash receptacle. "Except you're not stupid enough to want his phone number after that kind of treatment."

It did occur to him that cosmic payback was a bitch. That women all over the city of Miami—and probably the whole state of Florida—would find his predicament funny and satisfying.

The leather pants stuck to his legs in the humidity, and he again cursed himself for wearing them. But he didn't own a suit and the two pairs of dress slacks he did own were dirty. Dev shoved his aviators up his nose and reluctantly went inside to join the party, damp patches and all.

Kylie sat cool and elegant at a table three away from his, looking like a modern Grace Kelly. Not a soul in the room would believe he'd had her moaning in a utility closet. He almost didn't believe it himself.

He glowered at her from behind the aviators as he seated himself with Adam and Pete and the other groomsmen, but she didn't spare him a glance.

"What's with the shades?" their old college friend Jay asked. "Did I miss the paparazzi?"

"He's crying," Pete suggested. "He crashed and burned with the hot blonde over there."

Dev snatched the sunglasses off his face and shoved them into the breast pocket of his blazer. He turned his scowl onto Pete. "I did not crash and burn."

"Devon, I saw her walk away from you. I saw your mouth hanging open like a guppy's. So just admit it—you've lost your touch."

"Along with some of his hair," Adam added.

The table of guys erupted into laughter.

"Go to hell," Dev said, grinning and, in spite of himself,

putting a hand up to his head. Still bristling with frolicking follicles, thank God. "You're just bitter."

"Bitter, he claims!" Pete waved his fork. "Why, because in college, the Gig used to leave no women standing for the rest of us?"

The Gig. His old college nickname was very unwelcome right now. Dev ignored the hot slab of beef on his plate—it felt too much like a brother. He went to work battling the almond slivers that had slyly infiltrated the perfectly good green beans. Then he uprooted the parsley encroaching on his potatoes.

"I wasn't under the impression you wanted the women standing," he retorted. "So I left them on their backs for you."

Silence ensued.

"The sheer arrogance of that statement takes my breath away," Jay marveled. He was the writer among them.

"Good. 'Cause we don't want no stinkin' poetry out of your mouth, Shakespeare." Dev squinted at him much as he had at the duck.

"Wait, wait, wait. You're skillfully leading us away from the main topic," Pete pointed out. "Which is that *you went down in flames* with that woman."

More like up in flames. But Dev stayed silent. Why, he didn't know. He didn't owe her anything, not even privacy. But he kept his mouth closed.

Unfortunately every groomsman at the table simultaneously looked over at Kylie to evaluate the one female immune to the great Gig's seductive powers.

And she noticed.

Oh, hell.

She also heard the male laughter erupt once again, and saw them ribbing him. Judging by her frosty, disdainful expression, she assumed the worst: that he was giving them all a detailed description of the encounter in the utility closet—

and that he was doing so as some sort of payback for her not dishing out her phone number.

Dev slid down a few inches in his chair. Then he snagged a passing waiter and requested a gravy boat full of rum for his Coke.

RAGE PULSED THROUGH every nerve ending Kylie possessed as she sliced her filet mignon into ribbons. It was surprisingly tender, and she dragged each slice through a hearty lake of portobello/red-wine sauce before consuming it a little too ferociously.

Her sister Jocelyn and her husband Richard didn't notice, having eyes only for their son and his bride, and Mark's little sister Melinda seemed withdrawn and preoccupied.

Across the table, Aunt Mildred lifted a penciled-on eyebrow, but Kylie barely noticed. Through Mildred's beautifully swirled, spidery cone of hair, she saw Devon McKee guiltily avert his gaze from hers.

So Dev had initiated a regular *Penthouse* Forum over there at his table, had he? Why should she be surprised? She'd chosen him for his stud qualities, not for his maturity, diplomatic or social skills.

Still…for some reason, she'd expected better of him, maybe because he'd been man enough to apologize for his earlier comments. But clearly *man* did not equate to *gentleman*.

Mmm. And you've been such the lady this evening, yourself.

Kylie, unable to refute her conscience, simply worked herself into a greater rage. But it felt better than the depressive slump she'd been in lately.

"You're looking a little feverish, my darling," Aunt Mildred suggested. "Are you feeling quite all right?"

"I'm fine," Kylie growled, stabbing a forkful of green

beans. The slivered almond on top jumped to its death onto the plate in the face of her fury.

"You're sure?"

"Yes. Tell me about your cruise, Auntie."

Mildred brightened as she fumbled in her purse with something that rattled. "It was lovely, just lovely. We sailed out of Barcelona, as you know, and the next stop was Marseille where I purchased this darling little French sailor's hat, which would probably look better on you than it does on me." Mildred extended her bony hand and took Kylie's, forcing her to release her grip on her steak knife.

"What—"

Mildred released two small pills into her palm. "These will help with the cramps," she said in a stage whisper.

Mortified, Kylie ignored the smirks of the cousins to either side of her. "I'm not— I don't—" Dear God, could the evening get any worse?

Mildred smiled and nodded at her. "Take them."

"Thank you, but no." She didn't know what they were, and she didn't need them. Despite the fact that her head was beginning to pound, Kylie slipped them into her pocket, and took a large, fortifying swallow of wine instead. Then another.

She finished dismembering her steak and washed it down with more wine while the smirking cousins exhausted the subject of the weather and bravely broached politics. Finally, no longer smirking, they gave up trying to make small talk with her, and she with them.

The steak was followed by coffee that burned her mouth and a flan that seemed actively afraid of her, judging by its cowardly quivers.

Before Kylie could take a bite of it, her brother-in-law Richard stood to make a speech.

"I want to thank you all for coming this weekend, especially you out-of-towners, to celebrate this joyous occasion of

Mark's marriage to Kendra. When he first brought her home to meet us, I said to my wife Jocelyn, 'Kendra's the one.' She's beautiful, she's smart, she's a sweetheart. She's a lot like you, honey."

Beside him, Kylie's older sister Jocelyn preened, and all the women in the room sighed.

Kylie found her rage melting into sentiment and girly-goo at Kendra and Mark's happiness, and Jocelyn and Richard's, too. But all too soon, the girly-goo spawned a horrifying, shameful self-pity.

It could have been, should have been, Kylie's and Jack's wedding before this one.

Oh, stop it. Jack is a jerk. And surely, you are not this small and this mean. Be happy for Mark.

"Two years later," Richard continued, "here we are. So I was right! Then again, just ask Jocelyn. I'm always right, *right,* honey?"

The room rumbled with low laughter while Jocelyn lifted her eyes heavenward and said, "Yes, dear."

"In fact, I haven't been wrong since 1972, the one and only time I stopped and asked for directions. But I digress. Back to Mark and Kendra and their very happy day…"

Kylie looked at her wineglass as a tide of unwelcome emotion washed from her stomach to her throat and then receded, leaving nausea in its wake. If she could have dived into the wine and drowned herself in it, she would have.

She still remembered the two-foot-high stack of bridal magazines she'd once happily pored over, anticipating the day that she and Jack would celebrate their own wedding.

She also remembered how heavy they were when she picked up the entire stack and staggered outside to the Dumpster. She hadn't had the strength to throw all of them into it at once, so she'd lobbed them one by one into the big metal bin until her arm ached. She'd pictured all of those glossy, grinning, two-dimensional brides landing with satisfying splats in mounds of coffee grounds, eggshells and putrid leftovers.

Richard, bless him and his fatherly pride, was still talking. "I've always been proud of my son, from the moment he was born. I watched him take his first steps and I will never forget the day he wobbled down the driveway on his bike, independent of my guiding hand. Course, I'll never forget the way he forgot how to use the brakes, either, and plowed straight into our neighbors' pile of leaf bags…"

"Dad, please," Mark protested as everyone chuckled.

"But I've never been prouder of him than at this particular time, when he takes the hand of this lovely young woman and leads her into their future together." Richard started to choke up.

Kylie sympathized with him. She really did. Because the tide of emotion was back at her throat, too, and it rose steadily this time. There was no denying it, no pushing it back.

"So may I propose a toast now, to my son Mark and his beautiful bride, Kendra!" Richard raised his glass.

So did every guest in the room, including Kylie.

Then she excused herself politely and ran from the hotel.

5

As the first notes of the wedding march sounded the next evening, Dev stood with the other groomsmen, flanking a beaming Mark. The doors of the chapel opened wide to admit a white-clad, veiled Kendra, escorted by her father.

She looked beautiful in the dress, which had a V-shaped neckline filled in with some kind of fancy lacy stuff and short, poofy sleeves. Her waist looked tiny and the back of the dress dragged along the carpet, which women seemed to find romantic for some reason that he'd never comprehend.

Everyone in the church gave a collective sigh at the bride's stunning gown and radiant face. Her mother, grandmother and even Great Aunt Mildred produced white handkerchiefs and began their eye-dabbing immediately.

As for Mark, his chest swelled and he looked as though he'd died and gone to heaven. His eyes even held suspicious moisture. Once Dev would have made fun of him, but today... today he swallowed a weird lump in the back of his throat.

As the bride made her graceful journey down the red-carpeted aisle, Dev searched for Kylie among the pews. There she was, sitting in the second row back on the groom's side, with an odd expression on her face. It seemed loving and warm...

and at the same time forlorn. Her hazel eyes held a regret that seemed out of place for the occasion.

Dev had noticed her sudden disappearance after the champagne toast the night before, and fought the uneasy feeling that he might be to blame—even though he'd been a complete gentleman. He, Dev, the artist formerly known as Gig, the idiot who'd taken pride in the bra-festooned chandelier over his dining room table, had done his very best to behave.

Kylie met his gaze for the briefest of seconds before she averted her eyes and stared fixedly at the black-robed minister who waited for Kendra and her father to take their final steps to the front of the church.

What, Kylie couldn't even *look* at him? Dev's mild indignation of yesterday grew. It was one thing to use him then deny him her phone number. But it was quite another to pretend now that he didn't exist. He'd *existed,* all right, when she'd come for him in the supply closet.

And no matter what she might think, he had *not* given the guys a blow-by-blow description of what had taken place. So after the ceremony, he and Ms. Kent were going to have a chat, whether she liked it or not.

A naked chat would be better than a clothed one, truth to tell. As the minister droned on, Dev tuned him out and indulged some enticing memories of what Kylie's smooth, bare thighs looked like. And what that sweet little derriere of hers felt like in his hands. And—

"We are gathered here today …" intoned the minister.

To have impure thoughts in church? To pop a woody in front of God and all the guests? Get a grip, man!

Mark and Kendra held hands as the familiar words of the traditional ceremony echoed throughout the nave. They looked into each other's eyes. They smiled like a couple of drunk angels. It was—no other way to put it—sweet. And Dev had no doubt that the two of them would not lose that lovin' feeling. You could tell with these two—they'd make it through anything life lobbed at them.

Dev wondered if one day a woman would look at him like that: as if she'd gladly put her soul into a stew pot and serve it to him with hot, crusty bread. As if nothing would make her happier than simply to make him happy.

And he wondered, too, if he'd look at a girl the way Mark did at Kendra: as if he'd slay any dragon, shoulder any mortgage and work five jobs just to keep her in designer shoes.

Aw, hell. He was getting all whatdyoucallit, that German word for sentimental—*verklempt*.

"Do you, Marcus James Edgeworth, take this woman…"

Dev found himself staring at Kylie again.

Her gaze flickered over him and she moved in the pew, uncrossing and recrossing her legs. She didn't acknowledge him in any way, though.

Squirming, honey? If not, you will be soon. Because not only are you going to look *at me before this night is over, but you're also going to* dance *with me. Up close and personal.*

"Do you, Kendra Lynn Kirschoff, take this man…"

He kept staring deliberately at Kylie until he could have sworn she blushed, but he was too far away to be sure.

Dev turned his attention to the ceremony just as the minister said, "I now pronounce you man and wife. You may kiss your bride."

Up went the veil, down bent Mark's head, and it was a regular smooch-a-rama up there.

"Easy, boy!" said Kendra's father, and everyone burst out laughing.

Then bride and groom went traipsing down the aisle and out the door, followed by the wedding party. While people milled around, Dev lurked behind a partition in the musty-smelling hallway until he saw Kylie.

He greeted her affectionately as she passed him and slid an arm around her waist. "Need a ride to the reception?"

"No, I—"

"Fantastic," he said, grinning amiably and hustling her out into the parking lot.

"I don't want a ride from you!" Temper flared in those hazel eyes.

"Funny, you sure wanted a ride last night." He continued to tow her along while she balked.

"Oh!"

"So I find it *real* interesting that you didn't say goodbye, that today you won't make eye contact with me and that you seem to want me dead."

An ominous silence fell, until she finally retorted, "Alive. But in serious pain."

"Why?"

"You know exactly why."

"Nope. I don't. If your nice-girl-gone-astray guilt is kicking in, you shouldn't take it out on me. I didn't make you do anything you didn't want to do. I didn't proposition myself, tease myself or screw myself in that closet, Sweet Pea. You were there for every step of the process."

"This has nothing to do with guilt. It has to do with you being a jerk of *epic* proportions."

"Thank you for the compliment. It's true that my proportions have been described as epic. What I don't get is the jerk part."

"Oh, you get it, all right." She tried to pull away from him again. *"Let go of me."*

"No. We're going to have a little talk," he told her, stepping up the pace so that she tottered on her high heels and had to hang on to him for support as he towed her along.

"I have nothing to say to you, and if you dare try to manhandle me into your car, I will file kidnapping charges against you!"

"Don't be melodramatic," said Dev, unlocking the passenger door of his screaming red Corvette. "Now get in."

"No."

"What is your problem?" Dev asked, raising his voice on purpose as an elderly couple approached. "You practically raped me in the supply closet last night and now—"

Kylie whipped her head around. "Keep your voice down!"

The couple got a little bug-eyed but pretended not to hear as they shuffled toward their Buick.

"I'll be glad to whisper if you'll get in the car instead of behaving like the lead actress in a bad soap."

With a look that would have reduced a lesser man to rubble, Kylie folded herself into the low-slung sports car, showing a lot more leg than she probably intended to—not that he minded.

Dev shut the door for her and rounded the nose of the 'Vette to get in himself. "Now," he said, closing his own door and starting the engine, "just what are you so pissed off about?"

"You *know* why I'm pissed! You're disgusting. You're a *pig,* McKee. I saw you telling your buddies all about us."

"You saw nothing of the sort."

"What, do you think I'm stupid? You were three tables away, your friends were falling over themselves laughing, and you were all looking at *me!*"

Dev shot out of the exit, took the corner on two wheels and watched, amused, as she flailed for her seat belt. The powerful eight-cylinder engine made her breasts jiggle under the prim dress. Pig or not, he enjoyed it.

"For your information, sweetheart, the guys were laughing because they were convinced that you'd blown me off. That I tried, and failed, to get into your pants."

She finally clicked the tongue of the seat-belt fastener into the latch, then turned to face him. "Oh, but I'll just bet you enlightened them, didn't you?"

"No," he said evenly. "I did not."

"Then why were they all laughing so hard?"

"Because they loved seeing me strike out. It doesn't—" Dev shut his mouth abruptly, as self-preservation kicked in. It was probably best not to call attention to his man-whore past.

"Doesn't what?"

"Forget it."

"Doesn't happen often?"

Dev felt his face and neck get warm. "I didn't say that."

"You don't have to." Kylie crossed her arms over her chest and stared out the window as if she couldn't get enough of the strip malls, gas stations and convenience stores.

"Interesting. So does that mean you think I'm hot?"

A low growl came from her throat.

Dev grinned, then cleared his throat. "So I'm waiting..."

"Waiting for what?"

"An apology."

Kylie muttered something unintelligible.

"Excuse me?"

"I said, why should I believe you? It seems like an awfully convenient explanation."

"Are you always this ornery, or do I just bring out the best in you?"

"Well, it does!"

Dev sighed. "Pete saw the tail end of our first encounter, okay? The one where you said I might *do*. And he saw you walk away from me and out the door, while I stared after you like a brain-damaged sheep."

Her lips twitched.

"So he assumed that you blew me off, and he told the other guys, who thought it was hilarious that the one-time chick magnet crashed and burned."

"Chick magnet?"

"Look, give me a break. I was the lead singer in a popular band. Women threw themselves at me."

She tossed him a look of distaste. "Maybe I should have sprayed your *epic proportions* with the Lysol in the closet."

Stung, Dev said, "I used a condom!"

"Yeah. Maybe I should have made you use duct tape, too."

"Listen up, Miss Bee-yotch. As I recall, you were *begging* for it, and weren't too particular about whether I had protection with me or not!"

Her gasp of outrage was satisfying. "I went to the closet to *cry,* not to have sex with you."

"And I went to the closet to see if you were okay. Seems to me you're on some kind of emotional roller coaster this weekend."

Kylie shrugged.

"So what's wrong?"

"Nothing."

"C'mon, tell Father Dev all about it."

Kylie kept staring out the window.

"Unless you're just a garden variety psycho?"

"*That's it.* Stop the car and let me out."

"No."

"I'd rather walk to the reception than ride with you."

"The drama queen returns," muttered Dev, without slowing down.

"Stop the car!" she shrieked.

He rolled his eyes, made a last turn into the grounds of Playa Bella, the luxury hotel, and squealed to a stop under the portico, where a valet immediately came toward them. "Feel stupid yet? Would you rather I'd left you at the stoplight a block away?"

Kylie erupted from the passenger side of the Corvette like a blond hurricane, without waiting for the valet to hand her out. Dev was treated to the delectable view of her ass swinging furiously from side to side as she teetered up the carpeted steps and into the hotel without him.

He shook his head at the valet and shrugged his shoulders. "She had to get to the ladies' room, quick."

The valet's eyebrows shot up in clear disbelief.

"Okay, fine. She's late for a homicide," said Dev, scooping up the evening bag she'd left on the 'Vette's floorboard in her haste to get away from him. "And she really likes to be on time for her bloody murders. Pictures at eleven..."

6

KYLIE MUGGED A waiter the instant she was inside the grand ballroom. She snatched a glass of wine off his tray, almost unbalancing the poor man in the process. She drank it dry on the way to the buffet table, where she stabbed five Swedish meatballs, six mini-quiches, three triangles of spanakopita and an entire school of shrimp, which she drowned in cocktail sauce.

She stalked with her plate to the darkest corner of the ballroom, which happened to be where the huge amplifiers for the band clustered. Kylie maneuvered herself behind one that was almost her height and attacked her food like a starving goat, in the subconscious hope of filling the awful hollow inside her. She was four meatballs into the meal when she realized that she'd left her purse in Dev's ostentatious Corvette. Which meant she'd have to speak to him again. And worse, she'd have to do it politely.

With this realization came the full volume of the speaker as the band broke into "Endless Love," which presumably the bride and groom had chosen as the song for their first dance. She couldn't help it; she rolled her eyes.

Eardrums shattered, flushed from her hiding place, Kylie stumbled out from behind the monstrous black box only to run straight into Wilton Grubman, her older sister's best friend's son.

The two women had once forced Kylie and Wilton out to an eighth grade dance together, with disastrous results. Disastrous because Wilton had had a crush on her ever since then, and had been caught in the junior high boys' room doing unspeakable things with her class picture in hand.

"Kylie!" he enthused, his oddly triangular but puffy face beaming.

"Wilton," she said, trying desperately to dredge up a smile. "Long time no see."

Poor Wilton still looked like a possum. He had a broad forehead, long sharp nose and narrow chin which sat directly over plump shoulders as if God had forgotten that he needed a neck. Those shoulders transitioned into a barrel of a torso set on tiny legs. Wilton had small, pink, plump hands, too, that were always clammy.

"Care to dance?"

She was insanely grateful for the plate of food she still held. "Oh, um, maybe later? Thanks, but I'm starved."

"Here, let me hold that. You two run along and have fun," Dev said helpfully from behind her as he snatched the plate. She whirled to find him standing there with her purse tucked under his arm and an unholy smirk on his lips.

"Oh, no," she said sweetly. "I can't expect you to—"

"Of course you can! Listen—the band just struck up 'Shout.'" He popped her last meatball into his mouth and slapped her on the butt. "Go get 'em, tiger."

She plotted Devon McKee's murder as Wilton grasped her hand in his pudgy, sweaty one and towed her out onto the floor, looking as if he'd won the lottery.

Kylie was taller than he was. At every repetition of the chorus, he threw his arms up and hopped, morphing from possum to seal trying to snatch fish from the air. And her breasts were the fish, since with every "Shout!" they popped up, despite her best efforts to harness them.

That rat-bastard Devon laughed from the sidelines while consuming her shrimp.

Shout! Kylie decided to dismember him alive with a hack-saw and feed his limbs to a shark while he watched.

Shout! Better yet, she'd knock him unconscious, tie him up, smear canned tuna all over him and feed him to a herd of starving feral cats.

Shout! Or maybe she'd toss him into a mosh pit of violently vengeful women whom he'd spurned over the course of his career.

As the song got faster and sweatier and Wilton's enthusiasm for her even more oppressive, she contemplated the virtues of alligators, pythons and piranha, any of which were readily available here in south Florida and would satisfy her blood-lust.

Finally, the song was over. She dodged Wilton's determined attempt to slide a sweaty paw from her waist down to her ass, and thanked him for the dance. Then, through a series of dodges and feints, she lost him in the sea of people now filling up the room and made her way to Dev the Devil and her purse.

Her plate, she saw as she approached him, was a lost cause. It was littered with shrimp tails, quiche crumbs and flakes of spanakopita.

He waggled his eyebrows at her—for all the world like Belushi in *Animal House*—then popped the last corner of the only remaining savory Greek pastry into his mouth. He chewed, swallowed and smirked at her again. "Enjoy the dance?"

"I'd like my evening bag, please," she said icily.

"Are you going to hit me with it?"

"I reserve the right."

"Of course you do. So under the circumstances I think I'll hang on to it for a while."

"I'm not going to play juvenile games with you."

"Excellent," he said heartily. "Then can we move on to the adult ones? Triple X?"

She turned on her heel and walked away from him, toward a roving waiter. Somehow in three long strides, Dev got to the waiter first, commandeered a glass of wine and thrust it at her. "Drink?"

She ignored him and took a different glass off the waiter's tray. Then she continued walking while the waiter gave a mock-shiver. "Brrrrr. That was cold," she heard him say. "Why the hot girls so cold, man?"

"One of life's mysteries," Dev told him. Then, to her disbelief, he came up behind her again and touched her shoulder. "Don't you want your purse?"

"Of course I do, but I won't beg for it. I don't beg for anything, Devon McKee, not *ever,* no matter how you like to delude yourself about last night."

"Fine. Here." He extended it to her. "By the way, I put my phone number inside."

She snatched it from him and then hit him with it, hard, on the arm.

"Ow!"

"That's for eating the food on my plate." Then she hit him again, even harder.

"What the fu—"

"And *that's* for making me dance with Wilton Grubman!" She glared at him.

He said nothing. He didn't even laugh. He just evaluated her.

"What?" she yelled.

"Do you feel better, now?" Dev asked. There was actual concern in his eyes, and something appallingly like kindness in the curve of his mouth. It was horrible, unfair, the last straw. The convenient target of her hostility was being nice to her and that blew all her defenses.

"N-n-*no!*" And Kylie's face crumpled despite her very best efforts on behalf of Grace Kelly poise. Forget the minor leakage in the supply closet—now the waterworks started in earnest and great, wracking sobs overtook her body.

This should have been *her* wedding. She'd held in her emotions for eight long months, and now they wouldn't be denied.

"Oh, honey," Dev said, and folded her into his arms. "Oh, my poor little psycho…it's okay…whatever this is all about, it's gonna be okay."

His arms felt so good, so comforting, so right. How long had it been since a man had held her? The thought made her sob even harder as Dev walked her backward and to the left, and then backward again. She heard a ding and then they were inside an elevator.

"Not s'posed to be nice," she howled into his jacket. "S'posed to be a d-d-d-*dick*."

"I'm sorry to disappoint you," Dev said, with just a quiver of humor in his voice. "I do my best."

"S'posed to be a *d-dick* so I can *yell* at you!"

"I can see how my behavior frustrates you, then. I'm sorry." He smoothed her hair, which disarmed her further, which produced more sobs, except they sounded like wild hog snorts on the inhale. Which was even more mortifying, if that were possible—which it wasn't. But it was.

"So," Dev said, his chest rumbling under her forehead. "Is it me in particular that you want to yell at…or will any old dick do?"

She only cried harder. He couldn't possibly understand how painful the long months of withdrawal and rejection by Jack had been. How he'd changed under her very eyes from the man with whom she'd wanted to spend her life to a drug-addled internet-porn potato.

"I'm going out on a limb, here," he continued, "but I'm going to guess that you're very upset with some guy who isn't here right now…so you decided to use me as a stand-in punching bag?"

"I'm sorry," she wailed, punctuating the words with a great deal of mascara and—worse—snot. "I'm so sorry. You don't deserve this."

He actually kissed the top of her head. "If it makes you feel any better, sweetheart, I probably do. At least in terms of karma."

She began to laugh, then, on top of the sobs, because she figured he was right, but that didn't make her behavior any better.

She felt his hand cover hers, then take the purse back.

"I assume that you're staying here in the hotel?"

She nodded, smearing more makeup onto his jacket.

"And that you have a key card to a room in here?"

She nodded again.

"If you'd care to tell me the number, then I can push the relevant elevator button and take you there."

"Six-twelve," she mumbled. "Thanks."

He hit the button, keeping one arm still around her. She was amazed and grateful.

The elevator rose, thankfully without anyone else trying to get on. They stepped out onto the sixth floor and her room was only a few short steps away.

Dev slid her card into the slot on the door and opened it for her. "There you go."

She stepped out of his arms, feeling suddenly bereft, and went inside.

"Can I suggest a hot bath?" he asked.

Kylie smiled wanly.

"And maybe a bottle of wine from room service?"

She nodded.

"Okay, then." He stepped forward, took her chin in his hand, and dropped a quick kiss on her mouth. "Whatever this is all about—this emotional storm—it will pass. You're gonna be okay, Kylie. I promise." Then he turned and headed for the door.

The spiked hair with the gel in it that she'd thought was too Miami-stud yesterday suddenly looked right on him. His shoulders filled out the black tuxedo jacket to perfection, and the posture that she'd dismissed as cocky...well, who'd have known that it disguised real empathy?

"Dev?" she asked tentatively.

He stopped. "Yeah."

"How would you like to share that bottle of wine with me?"

He turned to face her, one eyebrow raised.

"Please?" she added.

He hesitated.

Perhaps it was underhanded, but she really didn't want to be alone. So she fixed him with one of those you're-the-only-man-who-can-save-me-from-certain-disaster looks.

"Hmm," he said. Not *yes*.

"I swear not to hit you with anything."

He grinned at that and seemed to relent. "Will you promise not to yell?"

She swallowed and pushed her hair out of her face, then struck a mock-sexy pose. "No. But I'll save it for when you get to...you know...the good parts."

7

DEV CLOSED THE DOOR behind him and leaned against it, shoving his hands into his pockets. "The good parts, huh. And what might those be?"

Kylie was, truth to tell, a woeful sight. Her nose was pink and shiny, her eyes red and ringed with black. But her mouth was still sexy, even under the smeared lipstick. And her vulnerability, especially after the whole ice-princess routine, did something funny to the male protective streak in him.

A smart man would have been so outta there, leaving not so much as a skid mark behind. But Dev had always been known more for his wick than his wit.

"You, of all people, Dev, know what the good parts are," she said.

"Show me."

She hesitated, but then reached back and unzipped the blue dress she wore, shrugging her shoulders out of the short sleeves and letting the bodice fall around her waist while Dev took in the smooth perfection of her unblemished skin and the bra that hid her breasts from him.

"Show me more," he suggested, his voice a little hoarse.

Kylie reached behind her again and unhooked the pale pink

confection, letting him look his fill as she slid the straps down her arms and let the bra drop to the floor.

D cups. Perfectly formed. Not store-bought. His mouth went dry and the pal in his pants saluted her small, budlike pink nipples—exactly the same color as the bra.

"How about the really good parts?" he asked, feeling a little light-headed. "Er, not that I'm complaining about these. They're…spectacular."

Kylie smiled and shifted her hips infinitesimally, so the dress dropped to the floor. She now wore very small pink panties, high-heeled silver sandals and…nothing else.

He had a very primitive, filthy urge to tear her panties in two and take her right against the wall. But he doubted that was what the lady wanted or needed right now.

What she required at the moment was care and finesse and seduction, so he told his inner gorilla to back the hell off and not even think about it.

Dev slipped out of his jacket and tossed it over a convenient chair. Then he unbuttoned his cuffs.

Kylie stood watching him, as if she were unsure what to do next.

"Take off those panties, honey," he drawled. "Will you do that for me?"

She nodded.

"Will you slide them down your thighs real slow?"

She hooked her thumbs under the lacy edges and shimmied out of them, her gorgeous breasts falling forward. He could see between them down to the line of her flat stomach, and as she straightened a little, all the way to the blond patch between her legs—a glimpse of heaven.

He sucked in a breath at the sight of the pink folds there, almost but not quite hidden. As Kylie brought the panties to her knees and raised one leg to step out of them, the view got even more erotic. He couldn't look away from the dark, forbidden crevices and the generous curve of her bottom.

Dev fumbled with the buttons on his shirt and ripped it off. Then he walked toward her, toeing off his shoes while he did. He removed his socks and then stood looking at those unbelievable breasts for a moment before he took them into his hands. Her soft inhalation of pleasure encouraged him, and he bent to kiss her.

Her mouth was hot, inviting and lush. Dev stayed there for a while, exploring the taste of her, enjoying her response. But he wanted to head south and taste something more taboo. He eased her into a sitting position at the edge of the bed, loving the sight of her in nothing but the silver heels.

"Spread your legs for me, sweetheart," he said. "Yeah... just...like...that."

She opened for him, quivering with tension, all pink and pretty. Dev sank to his knees and ran his hands up and down her thighs, loving her clear desire to be touched between them, but not indulging her yet.

When he did, it was with the very tip of his tongue. The delicate flesh there jumped, her pelvis jerked and she made a little noise in her throat.

He chuckled and touched her again while she gasped. Then he took a long lick, from low down to up high—and she let out a soft, strangled scream, her hips moving involuntarily.

He teased her mercilessly for a little longer before he went to work in earnest, but it didn't take long before she came utterly apart, crying out and thrashing and clutching at his head. He loved every second of it...bringing this beautiful, high-strung girl with the secrets in her eyes to passion and release.

When she opened her eyes, he unbuckled his belt, unzipped and slid out of his pants and then right into her, sheathing himself fully and groaning with the pleasure of it.

"Dev," she said. "That was incredible... Oh, Dev..."

He was a slave to his own pleasure, lost inside her body.

"Condom," she said. "We need a condom."

Nooooooooooo. His cock protested. He didn't want to leave the hot friction of her body. But he knew he was being self-ish. "Sorry. Damn it, I'm sorry." He had no right to take the risks with her health that he had taken with his own.

He pulled out and rolled off the bed to find his pants, his wallet. It seemed to take an eternity to locate the packet, open it, pull out the condom.

"Give it to me," Kylie said.

So he did. She crouched on the bed, leaning forward with her back arched and her breasts almost touching his cock while she rolled it on. He almost came in her hands at the sight.

He pushed her back down onto the bed, bringing one silver clad foot up and onto his shoulder. And then he slid back into her tight, hot body and gave her everything he had left.

KYLIE HADN'T THOUGHT it was possible for her to come again, but when Dev grasped her other ankle in his big warm hand and put it over his shoulder, too; when he pulsed in and out of her like some kind of human oiled piston; when he caught his bottom lip between his teeth and drove home with his hair falling into those sultry dark eyes and an expression of male exultation—well, she didn't have a choice.

The orgasm started low and tightly coiled in her belly. It stole all perception or thought from her and trampled them underfoot as tension built within her, spawning heat. Almost unbearable heat. Her consciousness spiraled into it and all focus went to sensation and friction in one spot—not the eager tip of her he'd teased and licked before, but some erogenous zone inside that exploded without warning and left her convulsing around Dev.

But he didn't stop stroking into her, and so the zone expanded and convulsed again. She heard a soft scream come from her own throat as a third minor explosion tore through her and sheer pleasure shook loose everything in her body.

Dev pounded into her once more and then turned his head and bit her calf as he climaxed himself, strangling the male groan in his throat. Her silver sandals still framed his face between her legs, his mussed hair, his fierce but exultant expression. He looked like some renegade sexual warrior. If only she could take a picture.

She must have smiled involuntarily, because he grinned at her. "I like the sandals, by the way."

"They complement your eyes."

"Don't make me blush."

She disengaged her ankles from his shoulders and lay like an exhausted starfish, still sprawled under him. "I think I should probably be the one to blush, considering the circumstances."

He chuckled and pulled out carefully, rolling to the side of the bed. He got up and went to dispose of the condom. When he returned, he stood looking at her, his fists on his naked hips. "I want you to promise me that you'll always wear high heels when we have sex. It's hot."

Her answering smile froze in place, and she closed her legs, pulling the covers up over them. *Always?* Always implied some kind of permanence.

"What's the matter? Is this where you tell me that you have corns or bunions or hammertoes and this is the only time I'll ever see you in heels?" His face conveyed mock-distress.

"No, no. Nothing like that. Come back to bed." She patted the mattress.

"Don't we have a wedding reception to attend?"

"How badly do you really *want* to do the electric slide?"

Dev rubbed his chin. "Good point." He rolled into bed with her. "Now, where were we?"

"I think we were just at the point where we were going to give each other naked massages," she suggested.

"How could I have forgotten?" Dev agreed. "I'll start with these." He took her breasts into his hands and rubbed his thumbs gently over her nipples, which came to attention immediately…along with every pleasure-attuned nerve in her body. She closed her eyes in bliss.

"These are incredible, you know. How did you come by them?"

She opened her eyes. "They're real," she said acerbically.

"I know they're real. I'm teasing you. You must have made a deal with the devil to get these from nature."

Kylie was a hundred-percent sure that Jack had first sought her out for her breasts, so she wasn't overly flattered. "Yeah," she said, rolling over and exposing her back to him instead. "I made a deal with the devil, all right. But not for those."

"Is he still in your life?" Dev asked, smoothing his hands down her back.

"Who? The devil I made the deal with?"

"Mmm-hmm." Dev began to work the muscles in her neck.

"No." Oh, his hands felt so good….

"What kind of deal did you make with him?"

"An engagement kind of deal," she said, as his magic fingers went to work on her shoulders.

"But you broke it off?"

"Yes."

"Can I ask why?"

"I wouldn't answer any of these questions if you weren't giving me the best free massage of my life," she said.

He chuckled. "Yep. I know. But I am, so…?"

"I broke it off because he preferred pills and porn to me."

"You're kidding. He preferred porn to *this?*" Dev had worked his way down her back and now had his hands splayed across her ass.

She nodded as best she could while he squeezed and massaged. Impossible, but she was getting turned on all over again. "Yeah. I guess I was too much work for him."

"Too much work," Dev repeated incredulously. His thumbs dipped between her cheeks as his hands slid lower. And then he stroked her where she was slick.

She moaned and let her face sink into the mattress as her back arched.

"He thought this was work?" Dev asked, as he put an arm under her stomach and lifted her to prop a pillow beneath her hips. She felt incredibly exposed, but forgot to be embarrassed when those clever fingers of his delved down again.

She muttered an unintelligible sound.

"What an unbelievable idiot," Dev murmured, and he bit her left cheek gently as he teased and rubbed her while her legs began to shake and the delicious tension he'd released before built again.

"Oh," Kylie said, as he slid a thumb inside her and yet stroked the little pink nub at her core with the pads of his fingers. "Ohhhhhhhh!"

"So we agree that he's a moron, right?"

"Yes!"

Dev was clearly some kind of contortionist, because he'd managed to get a condom over himself during all of this and now, with her wildly ready for him, he eased his cock into her from behind and wrapped his arms around her, taking her breasts into his hands.

The pleasure was indescribable and she could no longer formulate words as he rocked inside her and rubbed her nipples at the same time.

She didn't last more than five seconds and he laughed softly as she shattered around him. He seemed to get harder inside her and drove faster and faster until, with a last thrust that she could practically feel in her throat, he came with a guttural, heartfelt curse and collapsed on top of her, pressing her into the mattress.

Kylie was barely conscious, her pulse crashing in her ears.

"I'm so glad," Dev panted, "that you were engaged to a brain-dead Neanderthal. Because otherwise you'd probably be married, and I wouldn't have gotten this freaking lucky."

And for the first time, Kylie laughed about her broken engagement. She laughed until she couldn't breathe. She laughed until Dev had to give her some more mouth-to-mouth resuscitation.

8

DEV PULLED THE BLANKETS over both of them and tucked Kylie against him, spooning in the aftermath of sex. Lovemaking? It sounded so formal and odd. But *sex* seemed too casual for what he felt.

He stroked Kylie's hair back from her face. "Honey, you don't seem like the type of girl who propositions a random guy and gets it on in a supply closet during a rehearsal dinner. Or during a wedding reception."

"Um, thank you."

"So would you care to explain?"

She sighed. "Isn't it obvious, after what I just told you about my engagement? I'm hoping that a little sex with someone else will flush my system, so to speak, of Jack."

"And is it working?"

"Mmm. Very nicely, thank you." She gave him a cat-with-cream smile over her shoulder.

He took her earlobe possessively between his teeth and nibbled. "So you weren't thinking of this Jack-ass while my face was between your legs and my tongue was inside you?"

"Definitely not. He didn't like that much."

"Which only confirms my opinion of him as a complete

numbskull. Did you think about him when my hands were on your ass and my cock was in you?"

"Not once."

"How about when you had that triple orgasm?"

"Dev, are you asking me for an evaluation of your sexual performance?"

He shrugged, trying to hide a smirk.

"You were the best I've ever had. You're every girl's fantasy."

Music to a guy's ears, even one as jaded as Dev was. He lost the battle with the smirk. He preened a little. But then he frowned and lightly bit her shoulder.

"So you picked me to wash Jack-ass out of your hair," he said. "That was your hidden agenda."

Kylie shifted her legs. "*Agenda* sounds pretty cold."

"But that's exactly what it was."

She didn't answer.

"Just out of curiosity," Dev persisted, "why me?"

She sighed. "I don't know. You had the look, I guess."

"The look?"

"The hair, the gold chain, the leather pants, the reputation… Come on, Dev. You know what I'm talking about."

"Not really," he lied, somehow wanting to deny it all.

"Yes, you do. You look like a nightclub guy. The kind who goes out trolling bars for drunk, easy women in short, tight skirts. A one-night-wonder type."

"Are you calling me a slut?"

Kylie rolled to face him. "You're not getting offended, are you?" She touched his cheek with a manicured index finger.

"Yes. Yes, I think I *am* getting offended." He lightly bit the finger, now.

She pulled it back. "Please don't be. You asked why I chose you—and I'm telling you, that's all. You seemed like a guy who'd jump at the chance for uncomplicated sex with a stranger. And you did—so I read you correctly."

The more she talked, the more pissed off Dev became, probably because she was right. "Don't you think it's possible that you've misjudged me?"

She traced circles in his chest hair. "It's possible. You're much nicer than I thought you'd be. Much more understanding. But I'm a pretty good judge of character, Devon McKee. And I don't think my first impression of you was all that far off the mark."

Stung, he said, "What if I told you that yes, I've *been* that guy...but I don't want to be him any longer?" Dev stopped, amazed that those words had come out of his mouth, yet also dead certain that they were, strangely enough, true.

"Meaning what, exactly?"

Good question. "Meaning I want a real relationship. *Complicated* sex. A girlfriend. Someone to share my life with."

Aw, Jesus. Really? Where is this coming from?

The disturbing words were surfacing through the tide of self-loathing that ebbed and flowed within him. At low tide, he could stand himself, but at high tide? At high tide, he often ended up drunk and doing something that he regretted later.

"Why?" Kylie asked.

Why did he want to share his life? Hmm. Another good question. One that he wasn't prepared to answer, since it involved confessing his loneliness. "What kind of a question is that?"

"Okay, why *now*?"

Dev stared at her beautiful face, at the tiny lines radiating from her intelligent eyes, the determination under the soft contours of her lips. "Because now *feels* right."

"And why didn't it feel right before?"

She was a beautiful, blond Spanish Inquisition. Should he

confess his sins? "I was too busy being a hotshot to focus on anyone else, okay? It was all about me."

"So now that part of your life is over, you miss being the center of attention and you want someone to pass the time with?"

Ouch. Dev turned away from her and flopped on his back, staring at the ceiling. "Listen, Kylie—you're making me feel like some kind of criminal."

"Sorry. I guess I don't see you as the settling-down type."

Dev struggled up to his elbows and glared at her. "Hell, I didn't say I wanted a wife, two-point-four children, a dog and a white picket fence yet. I just want a girlfriend."

Kylie's lips twitched. "I've got some news for you, Sparky—at our age, most girlfriends are going to want the relationship to lead to something."

He laughed bitterly. "Right now I'm just trying to keep a fish alive," he said. "A lousy fish."

Kylie lifted an eyebrow. "How's that working out for you?"

"Truthfully? He looks like he's got fish flu."

She laughed. "Dev, really, don't take this the wrong way, but that doesn't bode well for the girlfriend."

He glowered at her. "What's so wrong with me? I have a past, maybe, but so does everyone. Just because I'm a relationship rookie doesn't mean I'll fail at it."

"I'm sure you'll do fine."

"So how about it?"

Kylie went very still. Then she turned toward him and sat upright, inching away and leaning against the headboard. "How about what, exactly?"

"I'd like to see you again."

She blew out a breath. "Look, this has been great. But it's just been sex."

"*Great* sex."

"Yes, but still only sex. And frankly, I'm not looking for anything else."

"So? You found it—me—anyway." He tried a big white grin on her. No dice.

"I just got out of a relationship."

"Just?"

"Well, eight months ago."

"That's not all that recent."

"To me, it is. I'm sorry, but I'm not ready to jump back into dating one person."

Undaunted, Dev took a different tack. "Okay, try thinking about it this way—have you ever bought a pair of shoes when you didn't need one, but ran across a great sale?"

Kylie let out an exasperated sigh. "Yes, but—"

"Or a hot dress?"

"Sure, but that's not—"

"It *is* the same thing. You may have found me unexpectedly and at a discount, but that's good fortune. Lady, you should definitely take me home. I'm one hell of a bargain."

"Devon—"

"Six-two, full head of hair, well-hung, no stock portfolio but I do own property—"

"Stop."

"—charming, tolerant of female foibles, mostly housebroken—"

"Stop!"

He stared at her, perplexed. "Is it my lack of a foreign language? If so, I can learn Spanish."

"It's not your lack of a foreign language, for God's sake."

"What's the matter? I'm not trying hard enough?"

"You're trying *too* hard." Kylie slid her legs over the side of the bed and walked to the bathroom while he gazed at her delectable ass.

"Well, why didn't you say so? I can do a fantastic sneering, son-of-a-bitch impression. See?"

The bathroom door shut on his best too-cool-for-this-world face. Dev sighed, dejected.

Dejection, like envy, was a completely new emotion for him. Another one he didn't understand. Devon McKee didn't get dejected. Depressed every once in a while, sure. For that, he had reason.

But generally, he was the life of the party, even when there was no party. He didn't envy anyone, because he'd always been the one envied. He'd always had it all—the musical talent, the looks, the lifestyle, the toys, the chicks.

Yeah. He'd had it all.

If only he could remember how and why *all* had fulfilled him. If only he could look back with less jaded eyes, he'd go down on his knees and gather up all the glee he'd spilled with abandon. He'd put it in a jar to be savored at moments like this one.

That past euphoria was gone with the wind. That sense of being king of the world. And all Dev had left were the memories, some old recordings and videos, and a pile of bras and panties.

True, every once in a while he got a small royalty check for a song played on the radio somewhere. And his sleazy sometime agent kept insisting that he was on the verge of closing a deal to use an old song snippet of Dev's for some TV commercial.

But that was it. He'd blown through most of his easy money, though thank God his father had made him buy some property. So he had his condo. He had his bar. And he still had his colossal ego.

Trying too hard? Him? Devon McKee?

Then it hit home: all those girls who used to run screaming after him, or conspire to get backstage to meet him, they'd all been so easy and available that he hadn't been interested. *They'd* been trying too hard. He'd taken them for granted.

And now look at him, practically begging Kylie to let him into her life. He was behaving like some groupie.

Disgusted with himself, Dev rose and found his clothes. He'd somehow ceded all power to her. He'd played the serf to her queen. Well, he was done with that, and done with her. Never in his life had Devon McKee not bagged the babe of his choice.

It was officially time to recover his inner asshole. Rake back some of the pride he'd scattered at her feet like rose petals.

Kylie emerged from the bathroom as he stuck one leg into his black silk boxers.

She looked at them as if they confirmed her worst fears. As if they'd been signed in blood by Satan himself. What the hell? Would she have been happier with a mallard print? He really was tired of all her disapproval. He was good enough for her to screw, but not good enough to let into her life?

"Dev," she said, in tones that held a stretched-taut kindness.

Oh, here we go with the Dear John speech.

"I think you're a great guy. I'm flattered that you'd want any kind of relationship with me, especially since you haven't exactly seen me at my best this weekend. But—"

He looked at her generous, glorious nude body, then cracked his neck. "Sweetheart, spare me the speech. I'm already over it. And if it makes you feel any better about being a psycho hose-beast, those tits overcame any personality flaws you might have displayed."

Her mouth closed. Then it opened again. Then it closed.

He put on his pants during the ensuing thunderous silence.

"*What* did you say?" she finally managed to ask in a voice

so arctic that it would freeze the piss of a polar bear in midstream.

He grinned at her and winked. "I said that your tits make up for your personality. Sorry, wasn't I clear enough?"

Her face went white and then strawberry-red. "Get out of my room before I call security."

Dev scooped up the rest of his clothing.

"You know," she said bitterly, "I'd actually started to fall for you. I might have called you in a week or two, if you'd backed off a little. But clearly, I misjudged your maturity level, McKee. Emotionally, you're still thirteen."

Thirteen? He didn't have to listen to this. Dev got his pants zipped as he reached the door. He yanked it open.

"Good luck keeping that fish alive," she called. *"Little boy."*

Dev slammed the door behind him.

9

IKE WAS UNMISTAKABLY DEAD. The goldfish floated on its side at the surface of his small tank, and if he'd had toes, they would have been turned up.

"I'm sorry," the neighbor kid sobbed. "I don't know what happened. I fed him every day, the way you said. Not too much, not too little."

Billy was nine, but looked more like he was seven. He was gangly, knobby-kneed. His round face hosted hundreds of freckles, his short red hair stuck out like the bristles on a toilet brush and the poor little guy was so upset that he'd actually fogged up his glasses.

Dev felt bad enough for him on a normal day—Billy didn't belong in some sterile high-rise with nobody his age to play with. But the parents were locked into a year's lease.

"Kid, it's okay. Really. We all gotta go sometime, and Ike had a nice life for a fish. Short, but nice." Dev handed him a tissue.

Billy mopped bleakly at his face. "You're not mad?"

"Nope. I promise." But truth to tell, Dev was as close to devastated as a guy with a dead goldfish could be. This, clearly, was a sign. An omen.

If a fish couldn't survive in his home, then how could a

relationship? Kylie's words echoed in his mind. *Emotionally, you're thirteen. Good luck keeping that fish alive, little boy.*

Dev stared at poor, dead Ike. How much easier and simpler to be a fish than a man…how much better. He cleared his throat. Better, that is, if you ended up in a decent home, unlike his own.

If Ike had been purchased by a worthier human being, he might still be popping in and out of his made-in-China treasure trunk. Dancing with the bubbles in his dyed-cobalt artificial reef. Racing joyously through the multihued plastic plants for the surface upon sight of his morning fish cereal.

But no. He'd been cursed the moment Dev laid eyes upon him in the pet store. That had been the *fin* de Ike.

Dev still remembered carrying him happily home in the plastic bag, poor Ike looking bewildered as he rode shotgun in the Corvette, sloshing crazily every time Dev shifted or braked. Then he'd calmed down while floating, still bagged, in the aquarium while Dev conditioned the water for him.

And look at him now. An empty shell of a fish, his joie de fishy vivre vanished, along with his giddy, gilly little soul.

Dev was damn close to bawling himself. Maybe he *was* emotionally thirteen.

"So," Billy said, sniffling. "Are we going to dig a hole for him?"

Dev frowned. "No. We're going to give him a Viking burial at sea."

Puzzled, Billy asked, "Ike was a Viking?"

"Well, not really. He wasn't the raping or pillaging type. But we can still give him a Viking send-off."

"What's pillaging? And what's ra—"

"Uh, never mind. It's not important. C'mon, let's find a suitable barge for Ike."

"Barge?"

"You know, a boat. The Vikings used to put their dead guys in a boat, light it on fire and then push 'em out into the water."

"Cool." Billy followed Dev into the kitchen, where he stood with his hands on his hips, eyeing the possibilities. Finally he settled on a paper French-fry packet from the trash. He cut down the side of it with a pair of scissors and trimmed it so that when he was done, it only stood an inch tall.

Billy ran home for a minute and returned with a yellow rose from an arrangement that his dad had given his mom for their anniversary. He peeled the petals from it and made a bed of them in the bottom of the little rectangle. Dev plucked poor Ike from the aquarium and laid him to rest.

They stood looking down at him for a moment, the mood lugubrious. Then Dev said, "Maybe we should give him some food for his next life, in the Viking tradition."

"Huh? Isn't he going to heaven?"

"Oh, yeah. Ike is definitely going to heaven. He might get hungry on the way, though. I don't know how long it takes to get there. Do you?"

"Nope." Billy shook his head.

Dev got the small can of fish food. "You want to do the honors?"

Billy shook out a pile of flakes near Ike's head.

"Okay, all we need now is a dirge."

"What's that?" Billy asked.

"It's a kind of song played at funerals." Dev went to his laptop and pulled up iTunes to find proper music for Ike's send-off. He finally decided on "30 Days in the Hole" by Humble Pie, and they marched Ike into the bathroom.

Dev set the makeshift burial barge in the toilet while Billy crouched next to it, fascinated. Good. Dev had done his job: to distract the kid from his guilt.

Next he lit a few of those candles that women called *tea lights*—why, he didn't know, since they had nothing to do with tea. Dev arranged them around the toilet seat and hit the dimmer switch.

"Got any last words for Ike, Billy?"

The kid furrowed his brow and pursed his lips. "Um. Well. 'Bye, Ike. I hope that you don't get hungry on your way to heaven. And I hope that they have Game Boys there and that you get to play. Oh, and we'll miss you."

"Ready?" Dev asked, lighter in hand.

Billy gulped. "You're going to set him on fire?"

"Yeah, just like the Vikings did. It's cool. Okay?"

"Okay. I guess."

Dev ignored the weird lump in his throat and reached down into the bowl. He got the little barge lit without burning off his thumb, and they watched it catch fire. "'Bye, Ike," he said softly.

Then he flushed the poor little guy.

The flaming fish circled the bowl faster and faster until the barge tipped, the whole thing fizzled and Ike was ceremonially sent down the crapper and out to sea.

Billy's lip trembled again as he blew out the candles on the toilet seat.

"C'mon, kid. Let's go get some ice cream."

DEV'S MOUTH TWISTED as he sat alone in his condo later, playing his old Rickenbacker for a wildly cheering shot-glass of Patrón. Buy a kid a strawberry ice-cream cone and chase away his demons in a flash.

Dev's demons, on the other hand, were here to stay. They sang the Humble Pie song with him again, and flickered with the muted television in the darkened living room. They swam in the first double-shot of tequila that burned down his throat, and the second, and the third.

The demons got into true party mode, though, when he inevitably put on the old video of Category Five's last set, the one where Wilbo was still alive, and playing this same guitar.

They'd performed on South Beach that night, on a raised stage on a patio behind an old Art Deco hotel a couple blocks down from the famous Delano.

The crowd had been wild for them, screaming the lyrics right along with Dev, acting like they were rock gods…Aerosmith or something.

Wilbo went nuts on the bass, playing with a manic energy even though the dark circles under his eyes were huge and his skin sweaty and pallid. He'd been drained and exhausted from a bout with mono that he'd never quite kicked, but this was their big shot to impress Ronnie Rizzoli, the head of TJX Records, who happened to be in Miami for a friend's fiftieth birthday bash. Ronnie had been staying at the Delano with one of his many girlfriends, but had condescended to stop by on his way to the party.

Before the opening set, Wilbo had been puking his guts out, and had then crawled over to the couch in a ratty cabana and lay prone on it.

"You okay?" Dev asked him, with only vague sympathy. "Because we can't mess this up. You know that, right?"

Will closed his eyes and nodded.

"You need something? A boost? Vitamins?" They both knew what Dev was referring to, and it wasn't a nutritional supplement.

"Nah, man. Got something."

Dev nodded. "You'll be okay. It's only one set, right?"

"Yeah," Will whispered. "Only a set." A rivulet of sweat ran from his temple down his cheekbone and then plopped onto the couch cushion. He didn't bother to wipe it away.

Those had been the last words Wilbo ever said to Dev.

Dev should have known. Should have taken him to the ER, or at the very least told him to lie there and not get up and perform. Who the hell cared that Rizzoli, the prick, was in the audience?

But Dev had pushed them all on stage, turned a blinding, egocentric smile on the crowd and soaked up the rays of the spotlights.

Devon McKee of Category Five hadn't given a rat's ass, ladies and gentlemen, for anyone but himself. They'd played a helluva set, that was for sure.

He sang a few lines of their hit single around a tongue that felt thick and half-paralyzed by tequila.

Gimme it all, gimme Miami Vice,
Gimme that hot girl—I'll do her twice!
Gimme the next one, yeah, I'll take a slice—
This is Miami, Miami Vice...

He'd been autographing a girl's bare breast with a hot pink Sharpie when Wilbo fell backward off the stage. He was dead before his skull hit the cement patio. His heart had stopped.

Dev didn't believe it, not even when the EMS team arrived on the scene and were unable to revive him. Will was asleep—he'd wake up any moment. Right?

Wrong.

Wilbo lay prone on the gurney, his hair askew, his eyes closed and his smart, sarcastic mouth weirdly slack.

Once EMS had come and gone, the cops arrived and asked a lot of questions. Devon answered them mechanically, as best he could. No, he didn't know exactly what Will had ingested, or where he'd gotten it, thank God. He wouldn't have been able to live with the guilt. Bad enough that he'd *offered* to get him something.

When the cops were finished with Dev, his first thought was to get to Will's parents before they did. They deserved to hear the news from a friend first.

He tore out the door of the hotel, barely registering that he'd barreled into Rizzoli, who was calling after him. "Hey, kid! I wanna talk to you."

"Not now," Dev said tersely.

He outran more cops on the way to Will's parents' home, when they tried to pull him over for speeding. But by the time he squealed his old Camaro into their driveway, another patrol car was pulling away from the curb.

He threw open the heavy metal door and ran for the porch without removing his keys from the ignition. Then he stood there, unable to ring the bell, his hands shaking and greasy bile burning its way up his throat.

In the end he didn't have to. Will's mother opened her front door and stared at him wordlessly with tears running down her lined face. Her eyes were bruises, shock pooling darkly under them.

"I'm sorry," Dev finally managed to say. "I got here as fast as—"

She drew back her arm and slapped him, hard, without flinching. Then she turned and walked away, her shoulders shaking.

Will's dad met her halfway down the hall to the kitchen, her white cardigan sweater and her purse in his hands. He looked at Devon with pure hatred in his eyes.

This wasn't the guy who'd taught him and Will how to play backgammon. Not the guy who'd cheered them on in Little League. Not the guy who'd picked them up, no questions asked, when at age fifteen they'd called him at 2:00 a.m. for a ride home from an area of town they had no business being in. And that, after sneaking out.

"You," the stranger who looked like Will's dad said. "You're the reason he's dead! Get the hell out of here. Get off my property."

Devon felt his face crumple and his lungs collapse. "I'm so sorry," he whispered. "So sorry."

"Yeah, you are."

I loved him, too, Dev wanted to say. *I loved him, too.*

But it clearly wasn't the time or the place. Dev hunched his shoulders and turned away. Took the three steps off the porch and into his new reality...which now included not one iota of ambition to be a big rock star.

Was it true? Was he the reason that Will was dead? After all, Dev had brought Will into the band, into the lifestyle that had killed him. Dev didn't know. He didn't know much of anything anymore.

He walked to the car, still idling, and slid into the driver's seat. Something in his pocket jabbed at him as he sat. He shoved his hand toward it and closed his fingers around hard plastic. Dev pulled out the pink Sharpie, recalled what he'd been doing with it when Will had fallen off the stage and threw up out the window of the Camaro.

DEV CLICKED OFF THE TV and bowed his head. His fingers played Will's bass line from the Vice song of their own accord as tears rolled down his face and dropped onto his T-shirt. Had he really told Kylie that her tits made up for her personality?

He had a hell of a nerve. Because the thing was...what made up for his own personality? What made up for who he'd been? Was there anything that *could* make things right?

He doubted it.

As Dev poured his fourth double shot of Patrón, his damned cell phone rang. He glanced at the caller ID as he hoisted the glass, and then put it down again.

Ciara, his sister. He may as well talk to her now, instead of tomorrow with a hangover.

"Yeah."

"How was the wedding?" Ciara had once had a crush on Mark.

"I'm fine, sis, thanks for asking."

"What did Kendra's dress look like?"

Dev rolled his eyes heavenward. "I don't know…white. With lacy stuff."

"Dev! Describe. Long sleeves? Short sleeves? Big and poofy, or sleek and sophisticated?"

"Uh. Short, poofy sleeves. Skinny waist, big skirt."

"What was the neckline like? Did she have a train?"

"A what?" He sighed, trying to remember.

"Did it drag in the back?"

"Yup. And the neckline was a *V.* Does that help?"

"Did she look pretty?"

"Yes. Kind of scrawny, but nice."

"Scrawny," she repeated thoughtfully. Ciara, like their mother, was well-endowed, and she was clearly relishing that Kendra was not. Women!

"Did Mark look happy?"

"No, Ciara. He looked like he was on his way to a funeral. Of *course* he looked happy." Dev blew out an exasperated breath. "Get over it," he added with typical brotherly brusqueness.

"Have you been drinking? Because your voice is kind of thick."

Dev glared at the phone and did the fourth double-shot. "Your head is thick."

"Answer the question."

"Maybe." Dev plucked the strings of the Rickenbacker.

"Liquor?"

"Get off my ass, Ciara."

"Playing guitar and drinking Patrón, I'll bet. Which means you're depressed."

"You've got me confused with someone else, sis."

"Promise me you'll put away the Patrón, or I'm coming over. And I'll go get Aidan."

Their brother. *"No."*

"Or Mami. I'll bring Mami. I will, Devon. I've done it before."

How could he forget their mini-intervention, during some of his darkest days after Will's death? His excitable, nosy Cuban mother, his dour, sarcastic Irish father, saintly Aidan and bossy sister Bettina—they'd all, with Ciara, announced their concern that if Dev didn't put the brakes on he'd end up like Will.

"Jesus, Ciara. I've had three drinks, all right?" Dev automatically subtracted one.

"Alone. And if you're admitting to three, they're doubles and you've probably had five."

"Four," he amended.

"So stop."

He was still sober enough to know she was right. Damn it. "Okay. Okay. Enough."

"Yes, *enough*."

"Fine!" Dev growled. "I hear you. Now bugger off," he said in a perfect imitation of their father's Irish accent.

"I love you, too. I'm calling in an hour, and if you don't answer the phone, I'll be in your face within fifteen minutes."

Dev hit the end button and grimaced. But a corner of his mouth rebelled and tugged up. Ciara was a pain in the ass. But it was always good to know someone cared.

10

KYLIE WAS STILL several miles beyond furious at Devon and pacing her apartment Sunday when the phone rang. If it had been anyone other than her niece Melinda, Mark's little sister, she wouldn't have answered it. But she adored Mel, so she picked up. "Hello?"

"Do you have a minute? Can I come over?" The girl's voice held trouble.

"Sure, if you don't mind my crankiness and Potsy's Seaside Delite cat food."

"I don't care. Why are you cranky?"

"It's not even worth going into, sweetie. Forget it."

Melinda arrived ten minutes later. She looked hungover and agitated, her dark hair scraped back into a messy ponytail and her blue eyes puffy and shadowed. "I hate my mother!" she blurted.

Kylie chuckled and folded Mel's plump body into her arms, giving her a big hug. "A lot of people do, honey." She felt compelled to defend her older sister, though. "She's all right, deep down. Just a little anal. She means well."

Mel emitted something close to a growl. "How does she mean well when she says horrible things to me?"

"First things first. Coffee? Tea? Wine? Chainsaw?"

Mel brightened at the last item.

"Kidding on the chainsaw," Kylie said hastily.

"Coffee, please." Mel followed Kylie into the kitchen. "Oh, God, what is that horrible smell?"

"Kitty food. I warned you. Potsy gets wet food for Sunday breakfast. He's spoiled."

"Ugh. Where is the little monster?"

"Sleeping it off somewhere—probably under my bed." Kylie poured them both coffee, doctoring the brew with milk and sugar.

They curled up on the rattan sofa in Kylie's living room, which was done in soft creams and beiges, with seashell accents everywhere.

Mel gulped half her coffee before saying another word.

"So what did Jocelyn say to you?" Kylie prompted.

"Basically that if I don't lose weight I'll never 'get' a man. And that I'm rude, ungrateful, horrible, et cetera."

Kylie sighed. "Start at the beginning."

"Okay…" Mel's cheeks pinkened. "Look, I had a really rough week. This jerk with a major account of mine, Franco Gutierrez, put the moves on me. Then when I declined his generous offer of sex in my bakery, he threatened me, called me a *gorda,* and said that I should be grateful he'd even think about doing me."

Men. Disgusting pigs. "Unbelievable." Kylie closed her eyes for a moment.

"So that's how my week started. I then got stressed about having to be around Mom at the wedding yesterday—you know how she drops her little comments."

"Mel, honey, they come from a place of love."

"Right," her niece said bitterly. "And Mark? He also thinks that if I lose twenty pounds my life will be perfect."

Kylie sighed. Sometimes she wanted to smack both her sister and her nephew.

"Anyway," Mel continued. "I drank a whole bottle of champagne by myself on the beach."

"Okay…"

"Then I kind of hooked up with Pete Dale," Mel mumbled.

"At the wedding?"

"Yeah." Mel's cheeks were flaming, now. "It just…happened."

Kylie thought about Dev and felt her own face heat. "Yeah. Sometimes it does."

"I'm not embarrassed about it," Mel insisted, though she clearly was.

"Why should you be? You're a consenting adult." Kylie reminded herself that she was, too. A now borderline-homicidal consenting adult. And she wasn't embarrassed, either. Nope. She sure wasn't.

Mel took an aggressive gulp of her coffee then set the cup forcefully on the table in front of them. "But Mom started needling me, and reminding me that Pete is an 'eligible bachelor,' and wanting me to throw myself at him. So I finally lost my temper with her and told her I'd already slept with him, thank you very much."

"Ah. And I'm sure that went over well."

"She basically called me a pathetic slut."

Kylie winced. "Oh, honey."

"And I was so mad I said some things, too. So now I'm an ungrateful brat. And worst of all—"

"Dear God, there's more?"

"Worst of all, Pete is trying to pretend it wasn't a booty call, probably because of Mark. He can't use then blow off his good friend's sister."

"Whoa, whoa, whoa. There's another possibility, you know, Melinda. He likes you and wants to go out with you."

"Right," Mel said. "I don't think so."

"Why not?"

"He's just being Pete. Mr. Nice Guy."

"Nice guys are few and far between," Kylie said fervently. "I should know. My last hook-up actually told me that my tits made up for my personality."

Mel's jaw hung open in outrage for a good few seconds before she snapped her mouth closed again. "What a—a…"

"Loser? Asshole?"

"Um, yeah. Both. Who was it?" Melinda demanded. "I'll go kill him for you. Didn't you just offer me a chainsaw?"

But Kylie was far too mortified to admit that she'd sunk so low as to have sex with Devon, let alone allow him say such a thing to her. She shook her head. "Nobody. Literally a pathetic *nobody* who thinks he's a hotshot. I won't even dignify his name by saying it."

"Do I know him?"

"No," Kylie lied. "He's someone I used to wash Jack-ass out of my hair for good." There. Saying the words aloud gave them more power. And she reminded herself that she had indeed used Dev, and not vice versa. Which gave his own nasty words *less* power.

She gave Melinda the best advice she could, did her best to bolster the poor girl's ego and told her to give Pete a chance— the chance that she, ironically, hadn't given Dev.

"But the bottom line, Melinda, is that today, we women have to take care of ourselves. Men aren't going to do it for us."

As the words came out of her mouth, she thought of Dev's surprising sweetness in the face of her emotional breakdown at the wedding. *Oh, honey. Oh, my poor little psycho...whatever this is all about, it's gonna be okay.*

Dev had, in the face of all the odds, taken care of her. He'd seen her to her hotel room. He hadn't even tried to take advantage of her. Huh.

McKee, in fact, had treated her a lot better than the nice,

stable, future Ward Cleaver she'd carefully chosen for a spouse.

Not s'posed to be nice, she'd wailed at Dev. *S'posed to be a dick!* She cringed thinking about it.

And he had, of course, reverted to her expectations later. The jerk.

So why did she feel so confused?

Kylie told herself sternly that she wasn't in the least confused. She was simply embarrassed. She didn't have emotional breakdowns in front of people. She'd dealt with the loss of both her mother and father at an early age, and life went on. There was no sense getting dramatic or messy about loss. It didn't change anything. Besides, Jack hadn't died. He'd merely knocked off her rose-colored glasses and stepped on them.

MONDAY FOUND KYLIE sitting at her desk in the loan department of the massive steel-and-glass Sol Trust bank building. The industrial air-conditioning vent directly above froze her neck solid and did a great job of cooling her café con leche within approximately ninety seconds of setting it down.

It helped her focus on her goals and banish the ugly emotions of the weekend. Goal: a perfect performance review. Goal: along with it, promotion to the next rung on the ladder for her, assistant vice president and group manager of her division. Goal: to be highly visible and seen as a shoo-in for eventual regional vice president of small business loans.

Around her buzzed the chatter of coworkers, talking to clients on the phone and to each other about the weekend.

Candace, the office gossip, had dirt on a married male manager she'd seen in a bar with a woman who was not his wife.

Alta, their resident earth mother, had brought in a coffee cake to share.

Face-time Gerald, who got to the office at 7:00 a.m. to be

seen by upper management and read news online, schmoozed with a client and offered to put together a foursome for golf.

Kylie tried to tune them out and focus on the paperwork in front of her, burning the numbers into her consciousness.

"Good morning, Kylie," said Priscilla Prentiss, her boss, from behind a huge stack of manila file folders.

"Good morning," Kylie replied, getting to her feet. "Here, let me take those for you. They look heavy."

Priscilla was hugely pregnant and the red dress she was wearing made her look like a giant strawberry. She was frankly adorable, even at fifty pounds over her usual lithe one hundred and twenty. Pregnancy was cruel to some women, but it became Priscilla. Her skin glowed, her dark hair shone and she smiled all the time, which Kylie found a little unnerving since her pre-pregnancy personality hadn't been nearly so sunny.

Kylie hefted the stack of files into her own arms.

"Thank you," her boss said. "Those are yours for the next three months. I saw my doctor yesterday, and he wants me on bed rest until the cesarean on Thursday. So I'm leaving a few days earlier than I thought."

"No problem." Kylie looked at the stack, refrained from gulping audibly and lowered the files onto her desk.

"I sent you an email with some dates to be aware of and other pertinent information. I know it's a lot to ask, but if you can familiarize yourself with all the loans in the next day or two, I'd appreciate it. That way, if you have any questions, you can ask me before I'm unavailable. There are a couple of businesses that need an in-person checkup soon—this week if possible. There are pink sticky notes on those folders."

"Sure. Of course." Inward groan. "So how are you feeling?"

"Great!" Priscilla already had a little boy, so she'd been through the drill before. Apparently she wasn't too nervous.

"Well, I've got a lot to wrap up. Thanks for stepping up to the plate on this, Kylie."

"No problem," she said again, even though the truth was that the plate had stepped up to her. "Let us know how everything goes, okay? We'll be thinking about you!"

"I sure will." And the giant, adorable strawberry returned to her office.

Kylie stared at the mountain of files. Well, she *had* offered to help out while Priscilla was on maternity leave. Although she'd expected to maybe split the job with one or two other people, not be saddled with everything by herself.

She sighed, feeling once again small and mean that she couldn't be happy for her boss and not mind all the extra work. But it would have been nice if the stork had brought a temp worker as well as a baby.

She took a sip of her lukewarm coffee and continued with her work, checking to see that all the documentation was there for this particular loan and tracking down the relevant pieces when they weren't. This part of her job wasn't very exciting. She much preferred meeting with customers, doing due diligence on their businesses and assessing the risks of the loans. But paperwork was part of the process.

Kylie worked steadily until lunch, then walked across the street to a deli and got a chicken salad sandwich to go. She was headed into the office when she spied Milty Goldman, the president of the bank, getting out of his silver Mercedes coupe.

Goldman was the very model of a senior bank executive: trim from playing squash, tan from playing golf, square-jawed, silver-haired and dark-suited with impeccably manicured hands.

"Ms. Kent, isn't it?" he greeted her. "Kylie."

She was pleased that he remembered her from the occasional meeting and company function they'd both attended. "Yes, sir. How are you, Mr. Goldman?"

"Fine, fine. And you?"

"Very well, thank you."

He nodded, then turned and reached into the backseat of the Mercedes for his leather computer bag. "I heard about your initiative to streamline the process for small business loans. That was very innovative of you."

"Th-thank you," Kylie said, taken aback.

"Keep up the good work." Milty flashed a smile at her as he shut the car door.

"Yes, sir." Flattered, she practically floated to her desk where the stacks didn't seem quite so daunting. They were still substantial and she knew the more she did in the office, the less she'd have to take home.

She unwrapped the sandwich and took a bite as she flipped through the information in the top file. The business loan had been made to a small family-run nail salon, and they'd used the money to finish the commercial space, as well as to purchase equipment like special pedicure chairs, manicure stations and a washer and dryer to keep the salon towels clean. Everything was in order.

She closed that file and looked through another one, in which the loan had been made to a greenhouse and garden center. Payments had been late a couple of times, which indicated that their cash flow was spotty, but overall the loan made sense.

Kylie went on to a third, this one bearing a pink sticky note on the front of it. Her boss had scribbled:

Guy is somewhat disorganized. Check to see that he's on track. Watch this one carefully and make in-person visit before okaying second installment of loan.

Hmm. She took another bite, savoring the crunch of green apple bits and walnuts, and flipped the file open. She was in the act of swallowing when her brain processed the name on the loan: Devon McKee.

Kylie blew chicken salad all over the wall of her cubicle. It wasn't pretty.

11

"KYLIE, are you okay?" Priscilla inquired.

Of course. Of *course* her strawberry of a boss had seen her spew. Murphy's Law had Kylie in its jaws like a rat terrier with a dirty sock.

"F-fine!" Kylie managed to say, clearing her throat and lunging at the mess with her napkin. "Just food down the windpipe."

Priscilla nodded. "You really should take your lunch into the break room, you know."

Kylie hunched her shoulders. "Normally I would, but I was trying to get ahead of these files and it's hard to concentrate in there...with four or five different conversations going on around you."

"I see. Well, all right then." She smiled. "Keep up the good work. We do appreciate it." Priscilla left Kylie to stare in horror at Devon McKee's neatly typed name, address and phone numbers.

She was being ridiculous. There were probably at least twenty Devon McKees in the south Florida region. This wasn't necessarily the one she loathed with every fiber of her being.

If it makes you feel any better about being a psycho hosebeast, those tits made up for any personality flaws....

But the cell phone number looked all too familiar. She had an almost photographic memory for numbers, and Dev had left those same digits, in that order, on a slip of paper in her purse. She knew this because she'd removed it to flush it down her toilet—after dumping the goodies from the cat box on top of it. Juvenile, maybe, but it had relieved her feelings.

Kylie stared at the file. This had to be some kind of cosmic joke. She didn't really have to go see the creep at his business, did she? Run through his figures with him? Check to see that the bank's investment was safe?

She didn't really have to share the same airspace and table while they talked? Endure the sight of him while he ogled her breasts? Surely God was not this cruel.

Her first instinct was to go to Priscilla and tell her that someone else had to handle this loan. But her boss had one thing on her mind: clear the decks so she could have her baby without worry. And going to Priscilla would lead to all kinds of unwanted, unanswerable questions. Plus it would make her, Kylie, look less than professional.

Which was completely unacceptable.

No, she was going to have to deal with Devon McKee somehow. There was no avoiding it. The bank had entrusted her with minding its money…no matter how much she minded this particular customer.

And he, in turn, was going to have to deal with her. If he so much as set a toe out of line, she'd shut down his funding and he'd have to serve corn dogs on a stick at his grand opening. The thought had her grinning evilly.

But the grin faded immediately as she realized that he could make things very uncomfortable for her if he wanted to. Kylie stuffed her sandwich into its wrapper, her hands suddenly clammy. What if he called the bank and told them that he wouldn't work with her, and why?

It could mean disaster for her career. Complete catastrophe. She pictured Milty Goldman's expression if Dev did that.

"Yes, Mr. Goldman? This is Dev McKee calling about the psycho hose-beast in your loan department? The one with the spectacular rack? Yes, Kylie Kent..."

She shuddered and dropped her face into her hands. No, she could not pull rank on Dev. She didn't dare.

Her fingers itched to call Melinda and pour out her own tale of woe, but she was too damned proud. She gave advice. She didn't ask for it. She was a self-contained unit, and had been since her parents had died.

Except when it came to Devon McKee.

How had her life turned into a nightmare?

A FEW DAYS after the wedding, Dev prayed for patience as he unloaded liquor boxes behind the bar at Bikini, his bar on South Beach. He was hot, sweaty and scruffy from two days of not shaving. His T-shirt was soaked through, since he'd been physically moving a thousand dollars worth of food and supplies from the back of his second car, a battered SUV, into the storage room.

Normally the kitchen staff might have picked this stuff up, but Dev didn't trust them with his credit card yet. Besides, he'd rather that they keep focused on preparing for the grand opening that would expand what was now only a club into both a bar and restaurant. It was a massive undertaking and one that would change his business.

Right now, on the weekends, Dev often hired beautiful girls in—yes—bikinis to lounge on or in front of the bar. So while the place didn't have an ocean view, it did have other views that were just as scenic—and more curvaceous. The problem was that they could also be high-maintenance and temperamental. It was always a toss-up whether their antics were worth the crowd they drew. Maybe once the restaurant opened and attracted its own crowd, he'd skip the scenery.

It was five o'clock, and Lila, his main bartender and another star attraction, was having a heated argument with her boyfriend instead of getting set up for the evening.

"Si tu tuvieras huevos y tu tuvieras un trabajo decente, yo no tendria que trabajar aqui in esta cantina de mierda y mostrar mis tetas!" She paced in front of Dev, gesticulating wildly but perfectly balanced on her five-inch black bondage sandals. She wore black leggings and a top that would be illegal in most states, deliberately pulled down low enough that a couple of centimeters of red lace bra showcased her assets.

Men flocked to Bikini to suffer abuse at Lila's hands. She made Dev thousands of dollars per night, so he put up with her temper, insolence and occasional laziness.

Her long, dark hair whipped behind her as she moved and her inch-long, dark red nails gleamed in the low lighting. Her lush lips drew back into a snarl, exposing blinding white teeth as she continued her tirade.

Dev knew enough Spanish to get by, and he discerned that the fight was about flirtatious behavior on her part. The boyfriend, Stefan, objected and had called her a slut. Lila countered by saying that she wouldn't have to work in Dev's crappy bar with her tits on display if Stefan were a real man and made decent money.

Dev winced on his own behalf as well as Stefan's. *Crappy?* His joint was a little downtrodden after years of service and several different reincarnations under different ownership, but it was *not* crappy. He'd done what he could to upgrade it, including ripping out the old bar and installing a maple one. The top of it consisted of a deep pocket that he'd filled with white sand, shells, sand dollars and replica fish, all covered by a thick piece of glass. Not bad if he did say so himself.

He slammed two bottles of Tanqueray into place, then the

Cuervo. He transferred more Dos Equis into the cold case that held the beer, and followed it with Corona and Tecate.

The restaurant in the adjoining space was going to be stunning…assuming that he'd bribed the electricians enough to actually show up in the next couple of days to finish installing the lighting, so that he could then bribe the inspectors to get the permits finalized. And the freakin' flooring guys to please, for the love of God, finish installing the toe-board and trim so that he could then rebribe the painters with beer to do the last of the painting.

It was all enough to drive him to drink…or worse.

Dev switched out the empty kegs on tap as well as the mixers, occasionally looking over at Lila to indicate that she might want to get off her cell phone and help. She studiously ignored him and cursed into the phone. Finally she spat one last doozy, hit the off button and stormed into the ladies' room.

Dev sighed. Unfortunately, he was used to this. He looked at his watch. Where were the cocktail waitresses? Angie and Marla shared an apartment and a car, meaning if one was late, so was the other.

In the kitchen, matters weren't much better. He'd hired a Swedish chef to handle the top-notch food that the restaurant would serve, letting the former cook go in order to balance expenses. Unfortunately, Bodvar thought it beneath him to serve potato skins or anything breaded or fried—essentially the entire bar menu. The very smell of such *offal* sent him into orbit.

In an attempt to keep Bodvar happy, Dev had commandeered one of the sous chefs, Maurizio, to handle the orders. But since he had taken the job in order to learn the culinary arts from a master, Maurizio was now in a snit and Bodvar complained bitterly about not having proper support.

Dev was ready to attack the sous chef with a cheese grater

and hang Bodvar with the beef in the huge walk-in fridge. Instead he joked with them and went heavy on the back-slaps.

And then there were the new waiters to finish training. Two of them had a lot of experience, but the other two were wet behind the ears. Dev prayed that they'd work out under the tutelage of the older ones.

He'd been praying a lot lately, since so much was at stake. He was sure he could bribe, cajole and charm everyone enough to pull off the grand opening party, but they had to maintain rigorous standards after that. Too bad *rigorous* and South Beach didn't exactly go arm in arm. *Hot, steamy, salty, sexy, languid...*all those adjectives applied to South Beach. The trick was to keep enough of the beautiful crowd on your premises to attract the regular crowd and any tourists you could snag as well.

The beautiful crowd required pampering to show up. Free drinks and spa discounts and goody bags and everything else. It was enough to bankrupt a guy...speaking of which, he should call Sol Trust and confirm the second installment of the loan with that Priscilla woman. He'd tell her that he'd confirmed the attendance of Milan and Cheri, the very notorious, very blond twin heiresses to a hotel chain. And they'd bring all their friends, and the friends would bring friends...

Oh, thank God. Lila had come out of the ladies' room with fresh lipstick on, just in time to take the orders of two dazzled tourist guys whose tongues now dragged on the bar in front of her cleavage.

And that blue streak past the open front door had been Angie and Marla's Mazda, he was sure of it.

Dev nodded at the tourists and moved to get the last box out of Lila's way. It contained frozen chicken breasts and was covered with the brand name and logo of a well-known poultry company. Dev picked it up and turned to take it into the restaurant side.

That was when he saw Kylie, dressed in a navy blue pencil skirt, modest white blouse and pearls. She sported a soft-sided leather briefcase and an austere version of her mysterious Swiss bank-vault smile.

"Hi, Dev," she said. "I'm your new account manager from Sol Trust."

12

KYLIE LOCKED HER knees so they wouldn't shake and braced herself for Dev's reaction. It made her feel better when he fumbled the box he held.

He smelled a little ripe, but he was nothing short of devastating with a couple of days' worth of growth on his cheeks and chin. His damp T-shirt clung to every inch of hard chest, straining pecs and flat abdomen.

Lightning streaked through her as she remembered exactly how his face had looked between her thighs.

Dev cocked his head and quirked his mouth. "Ha. That's a good one, Kylie. Tell me another."

He walked past her, toward the back and then right, carrying the crate. He depressed a handle on a metal door with his elbow then opened it, holding the box one-handed with his knee bracing the underside.

She followed him, her high heels sounding like gunshots on the floor.

Dev disappeared inside what looked like a giant, walk-in refrigerator with floor-to-ceiling shelves. She caught up as he set the box down and distributed the contents onto them. When he turned, Kylie gave him a tight smile.

The door of the big fridge closed behind them automatically.

"I'm not kidding, Dev. I work in the loan department at Sol Trust. I'm your new account manager."

Dev's expression said that she worked in hell, as a misery manager, instead. "What happened to Priscilla What's-Her-Face?"

"My boss? She went out on maternity leave."

He wiped his filthy hands on the legs of his jeans. Then he pulled a utility knife out of his pocket, flipped the cardboard box over and sliced along the seams before folding it down. "Well, then. I guess you'll *have* to give me your number now." He laughed without much mirth.

A tense silence followed. Kylie felt her face flaming, even though she'd begun to shiver in the cold. Dev seemed unbothered by it.

Then he said, "I owe you an apology. I shouldn't have said what I did to you, but my ego was bruised."

Oh. Wow. Was there anything, *anything* sexier than a man who could apologize when he was wrong? It disarmed her. Just like that, all of her righteous indignation at him evaporated.

"Look," she muttered, "I'm sorry, too, that we got off on the wrong foot—"

His eyebrows rose along with the rest of him. He still held the knife loosely in his fist as he lounged lazily against the shelves, looking like an outlaw. The bare lightbulb overhead caught the blue highlights in his hair, and emphasized the drama of the growth on his cheeks.

The curve of his lips, sensual to begin with, deepened into something truly sinful. "Oh, I seem to remember that we got off, all right. Off *both* feet." He laughed softly.

Despite another shiver, Kylie flushed hot with mortification and unwelcome, recurring longing.

Why couldn't she decide whether she liked or hated this guy? Sorry one minute, sexually harassing her the next. He knocked her completely off balance. And he was probably worse than Jack on so many levels.

She wished she didn't remember every inch of Dev naked. "We're going to have to put that behind us, because there's no other option."

He retracted the knife's blade and shoved it into his pocket. Then he folded his arms across his sweaty chest. The grin hadn't faded. "But I'd so much rather get behind *you* again."

Images flooded her mind, X-rated ones, followed by re-membered sensations. His hands on her hips, holding her in place for him. His hands on her breasts, possessing them. His chest against her spine. Him inside her.

She sucked in a breath. The heat in her cheeks was nothing now, compared to the heat under her prim navy skirt. His audacity stole her words, dried her mouth. She moistened her lips with a tongue that felt like sandpaper. "You're a bastard," she said in low tones.

"I know," he whispered, moving into her space. His eyes crinkled at the corners in an unfairly sexy way. "I'm a dirty bastard to remind you of how much you loved it."

She shook her head. Her hands itched to slap him, but she held one fisted at her side and the other curled around the strap of her briefcase.

He stepped closer, and she could feel his breath on her face. "Admit it," he said.

She closed her eyes to block out his face: the knowing dark eyes, the clever mouth, the cheekbones that did unlawful things to her knees.

Felt his fingers trailing along her jaw and into her hair, stroking her ear. Her body, damn it to hell, betrayed her by trembling.

"Admit it," he said again.

She shook her head. She wouldn't give him the satisfaction.

So he kissed her. It was an act of sheer sensual aggression, the commandeering of her mouth as his playground. And in spite of knowing full well what he was doing, she couldn't help but respond to him.

He kissed her to make her open to him, sent his tongue marauding to find hers, to stroke it and gentle it into behaving. There was nothing violent in the kiss, but it was possessive as hell and she hated herself for the tiny moan that escaped her throat.

He made a noise of male satisfaction, pulled away and stroked her cheek. "Yeah," he said a little raggedly. "I got your number, honey."

She struggled to pull herself together, but his body heat enveloped her, as did his scent. He wore no leather today, but somehow he still smelled faintly of it under the musk of exertion. "You want me," he said. "Same as I want you."

What she *wanted* was to push him away, and at the same time, she wanted to yank up his shirt and lay her cheek against his chest. Climb him like a tree.

She felt like a crazy woman. She *was* a crazy woman. She should never have been in a closet with this guy to begin with, and now she was in a *refrigerator* with him?

Sure enough, there were crates of tomatoes and boxes of asparagus, bins of mushrooms and stacks of cheeses. Containers of sour cream stared at her, lined up with mayonnaise and milk.

The sheer incongruity of it almost made her laugh, except the situation wasn't funny.

She fought for what was left of her breath and made a declaration. "We can't do this, Dev."

Since he showed no inclination to move, she put her hands flat on his chest in order to push him out of the way. No dice.

"Why not?" he asked in reasonable tones.

"Because…because…we just can't. There's a moral issue at stake."

He smiled down at her. "Oh, I assure you that everything I want to do to you right now is completely *im*moral."

Her heart lurched and hopped, behaving like a mutant frog. Or was she confusing her heart with her— Never mind. That hard, hot pulse was *every*where.

"Some of it might even be illegal," he mused.

"Dev—"

"And impossible. But that doesn't stop me from thinking about it." He waggled his eyebrows, leering at her.

"Okay, really—"

"That pearl necklace of yours has me wanting to add to it, if you know what I mean."

God help her, she knew exactly what he meant, and more X-rated images flashed before her eyes. A naked Dev straddling her, sliding his cock between her—

"Dev, *stop it!*" She was afraid she might explode; blast off like a female rocket, leaving nothing but her damp, charred panties behind.

"What's the matter, sweetheart? You're sounding a little strained."

She glared at him, letting her eyes travel deliberately to his crotch. "Am I? Well, it's your fault. And you appear to have shoved a cucumber down your shorts, you jerk. You're no better off than I am."

He flashed white teeth at her. "Cucumber? More like a giant butternut squash, darlin'."

She slid away from him and made for the door. "You're impossible. I'm here on *business*."

"And like I said, I'm all too ready to give you the business."

She turned her back to the exit. "Do you ever think about anything besides sex?"

He eyed her as if he were starving and she were a slice of key lime pie. "Not when it comes to you."

The door was frigid and she pressed against it for relief from the heat of her own body.

"Well, get over it. Seriously. Snap out of it. Because I have a job to do, here, and you're going to have to help me do it— *with your clothes on.* Mine, too."

Dev sauntered toward her and instinctively she tried to back up, but had nowhere to go. "Me, I've always been a big fan of naked account management."

"No. No, no, no. No naked account management. Not happening."

He chuckled and kept coming for her.

"Stop right where you are, or I'll—" She didn't know what she'd do. But the threatening tone was good.

"You'll what, babe?"

She cast about for a sufficiently dire consequence.

"What will you do?" he taunted softly. He stood a foot away, looming over her. "Spontaneously combust?"

Yes. "Of course not."

His leer was back—not that it had ever truly gone away.

"Don't you lay a *finger* on me, or I *swear* I will—"

"Hump my leg?" Dev was openly laughing now, and she didn't appreciate it one bit.

Game over. "I'm leaving," she said, feeling wildly around for the door handle.

"No, you're coming," Dev told her. Then he leaned over and bit her nipple, right through the white blouse and her bra.

"Ohhh!"

Worse, he took the placket of her shirt in his teeth and ripped open the snap buttons, holding his hands in the air to demonstrate that he *hadn't* laid a finger on her.

Then, still using his teeth, he tugged down the edge of her

bra and captured the other nipple in his mouth, triggering chaos throughout her nervous system.

She leaned weakly against the steel door and gave in to the hot, sucking pleasure. Gave in to that clever mouth and Dev's utterly stubborn, wily, no-hands seduction.

He gave equal attention to her other breast before making a suggestion that was just short of a command. "You should pull your skirt up, now."

"I should?"

Dev dropped to his knees in front of her, still keeping his hands idle. "I think it's a real good idea, unless you want me to chew it off."

She met his gaze. She shook her head ruefully. He raised a completely corrupt eyebrow and waited her out. Still holding his gaze, she reached for the hem of her skirt and pulled it up, past her knees, and slowly up her thighs.

Dev nodded encouragingly.

She hesitated as she got to the apex.

"C'mon," he said. "All the way."

She pulled it to her waist.

And Dev bent forward and slipped his tongue under her thong.

13

KYLIE ALMOST COLLAPSED against the door as Dev touched her there, pressed his face between her legs. Pleasure took over and all conscious thought fled. The sense of the forbidden, the knowledge that discovery could be imminent, only heightened the sensations.

The two days' growth on his cheeks and chin abraded her inner thighs, but she didn't care. She rode the sensations, climbing higher and higher...

Until he took his mouth away.

She made a small noise of protest and squirmed.

"Kylie," he said, his voice husky. "You like this?"

"Yes! Don't— Please..."

"You don't want me to stop?"

"No..."

He did something incredible and her knees buckled.

"Okay, then you have to agree to a date with me."

"C-can't."

Dev did some kind of swirl or figure eight in just the right place and she clutched at his hair.

"One date," he insisted.

"You...are...the devil..."

"What can it hurt?"

"Aaahhh!" She was pretty sure he'd traced a question mark this time.

"Nobody has to know."

Now a heart? "Yes…whatever you want…okay…"

"Atta girl."

And Dev went for the kill as a reward.

She wasn't sure what he did, but she was *way* past analyzing it, a slave to heat and sensation, to rhythm and pure, unadulterated pleasure.

She spasmed, convulsed and came hard against him, over and over.

Dev chuckled and sat back. "Don't look, ma," he said. "No hands."

She came back to earth and was immediately embarrassed, since she was half-naked with her skirt rucked up around her waist, while he was sitting there fully clothed and getting an eyeful. Shaking partially from cold, she pulled her panties into place and yanked her skirt down.

"Hey," he protested. "You just spoiled my view…and besides, I have other plans for you, my pretty." He indicated the tent in his jeans.

"Dev, anyone could walk in here at any moment," she said, adjusting her bra and pulling her blouse together again.

"I know." He seemed unfazed by the concept. "That's what makes it fun."

"Fun for you. Catastrophic to my career." What was she doing in here? She could lose it all. Everything she'd ever worked for. And her job *was* everything to her, since her parents had died on her and her personal life had disintegrated. Maybe she'd round out her life by meeting the real Mr. Right one day and pop out a couple of troubled kids. But Dev was most definitely not that guy.

He stood up and took her hand, placing it on his erection.

"You're not gonna make me walk around with this, are you? You can't be that cruel."

It *would* be cruel. But Kylie feared discovery. She struggled with herself. So Dev wasn't Mr. Right. Why not enjoy Mr. Wrong for the moment?

She sighed. "Do you have an office in this place? One with a locking door?"

"Yeah, but it's about as big as a shoe box."

She shrugged and made up her mind. "Then," she said in her best Mae West voice, "why don't you take the big, bad, bank lady in to look at your books?"

"Mmm. I can't wait to adjust the figures." Dev pressed her against the door and set his mouth on hers, grinding himself into the hollow between her legs.

She wrapped her arms around him wholeheartedly and kissed him back. It surprised her, but she found herself actually *wanting* to go on a date with him, even if he'd used a low-down, dirty bribe to secure it.

She pulled back away in order to point out just how slimy that had been, and her left elbow connected with something solid—the lever of the door handle. It depressed, as designed to do.

And the door opened, as *it* was designed to do.

Kylie shrieked as she fell backward out of the walk-in fridge, with Dev on top of her.

Shit! Dev didn't have time to roll under her before she hit the concrete, but he got his arms under her head to protect her. Pain immobilized him as his elbows and wrists took the brunt of their impact.

"Christ, are you okay?"

Kylie evidently had hit hard enough that the wind got knocked out of her, because her mouth was open but no sound came out after her initial scream.

"Kylie? Hey, Kylie." He twisted onto his side to get a better view of her face.

Finally she gasped—once, twice—then closed her eyes. "My tailbone," she said. "Oh, God. It hurts."

Worst thing she could have landed on. He ignored his own pain. "Can you move?"

"Argh." She struggled to sit up normally, but it must have been too painful. She, too, rolled onto her side to take inventory. "Yes. I think so."

Dev breathed a sigh of relief, and the room came into focus around him. Along with three employees and their bemused expressions.

Bodvar held a long, wicked-looking chef's knife and half a chicken. Maurizio, the sous chef, wielded a spatula. And Marla the cocktail waitress clutched a corkscrew and a sweating bottle of white wine.

"Hi, guys," Dev said. He cleared his throat. "Um. They should put a warning on those fridge doors. They're downright dangerous. This is Ky—"

"Katherine." Kylie overrode him fiercely. "Katherine Jones. From, ah, the health department."

"Right." Dev rubbed his forearms. "So. Katherine, here, was inspecting the cleanliness of our refrigeration unit."

"Yes." She smiled brightly. "And I want to congratulate you all on a job well done. Extra points for tidiness. Although you may want to consider, uh, alphabetizing the contents."

None of his three employees was buying the act.

In his heavily accented English, Bodvar said, "Ya. Well. I get back to *de*-boning." He shot them a pointed glance, shook the chicken, turned on his heel and walked away.

Maurizio smirked, shook his finger and made a spanking motion with the spatula.

Marla pursed her lips and ran her hands up and down the wine bottle suggestively. "I'd better pour this before it gets too warm." But she made no move to leave, eyeing them with open curiosity.

"So nice to meet you all," Kylie said, then looked at her watch. "Oh! Boy, am I late for another appointment." She got to her knees and winced, clutching at her tailbone.

Dev shot to his feet and extended an arm to her, pulling her up the rest of the way. "But we have all that paperwork to fill out," he said, eyeing her meaningfully.

Her smile became fixed. "Paperwork? No, no. You can do that on your own. Mail me the forms when you're done." She tried to pull her hand out of his, but he hung on. He wasn't going to let her get away this easily. He was too horny. And he needed to cement that date with her.

It wasn't like he sat around and analyzed his feelings, but when he'd seen her again his brain had formed the word *yes*.

This is the girl. You screwed things up; now unscrew them. This is the girl.

"I can't mail you the forms. I have a few questions."

"Oh, it's all self-explanatory." The smile had become a simple baring of teeth.

Dev nodded and released her hand. "Fine," he said smoothly. "Then I'll contact you at work if I run into any snags, okay?" He bared his teeth right back at her.

Something like panic crossed her face, and a small tic started at the corner of her left eye. She glanced at her watch. "Um. I probably have a couple of minutes to spare. I seem to have misread my watch."

"Easy to do." Dev kept his tone agreeable to a fault. "Watch faces these days are just so complicated."

Her hazel eyes smoldered and promised retribution, but she allowed him to place an arm around her shoulders.

"Here, let me show you the way." Dev raised his eyebrows at Marla and Maurizio. "I'm sure the bar is getting busy by now."

They got the hint and vanished, leaving him and Kylie alone.

"First," she said in dangerous tones, "you play unbelievably dirty."

"Dirt is my middle name, sweetheart."

"Second, whatever you had in mind for me is not going to happen right now, because I can't even stand up straight. I think my tailbone is broken."

He seriously doubted it. "If it was broken, you wouldn't be mobile. Here," he said with a lascivious grin, "why don't you let me rub it for you?"

"Funny. Look, I don't know what you do all day, but I actually work for a living, and if I don't get back to the office, they're going to wonder what happened to me."

"And will you tell them?" He deliberately let his eyes roam her body. "Will you gather the girls around the water cooler and describe exactly what I did?"

"No, you pervert. You wish."

He laughed openly at her outrage. Her blond hair was mussed and he'd smeared her lipstick. Her white blouse had a big smudge on the back from the floor. Her skirt was a little worse for the wear, sporting a sea of suspect wrinkles. It didn't take an investigator's license to figure out that it had been bunched around her waist.

She all but advertised the fact that she'd been pleasurably manhandled.

And he was just the man to handle her. "I think you should probably go home and change before you go back to work."

She looked down at herself in dismay.

"Sorry." He offered her a sheepish smile. "I'm a sex-crazed barbarian. Your skirt never had a chance."

She sighed. "And I'm stupid."

"Right. Which is exactly why you're going out with me on that date we negotiated. How about this Saturday?"

She narrowed her eyes. "What if I said I was busy?"

"And what if I didn't believe you?"

"Why not? I'm no dog. I could have a hot date lined up."

"But you don't," Dev said with finality. "Or you wouldn't have come on to me at Mark's wedding."

Kylie inspected her shoes, seeming fascinated with the navy bows on the toes.

"So on Saturday," he continued, "how about if I pick you up at seven o'clock? We'll go for drinks at the Rusty Pelican and I'll make a dinner reservation somewhere."

She caught her upper lip between her teeth. "So this is a real date?"

"No, it's a fake one," he retorted, exasperated.

"How many other women are you dating?"

He stared at her. "None."

"Well, you need to find some and ask them out."

Dev glowered down at her. "Let me get this straight. You're *ordering* me to date other women."

She nodded.

"Next you'll want me to send you written reports on these dates, right?" He couldn't rein in his sarcasm.

"Don't be ridiculous, Dev. All I'm saying is that we can't get serious—"

He stepped over to the wall and literally banged his head on it. Once, twice and then a third time. "Serious?" he asked. "Nothing about this whole situation is serious, honey, so if I were you, I wouldn't worry about it. This is all one big, freakin' comedy. In fact, it's a farce."

14

KYLIE WAS AT HER CONDO before she realized that she and Dev had not discussed one thing about his business or the loan. Great. Just great.

The mirror told its tale: she looked like some crazed slut on a bender, or at the very least a character straight out of a disaster movie. What got *into* her when she was around Devon? She wasn't some idiot groupie, but somehow she degenerated into one as soon as he shot her those teasing, smoldering looks of his.

She stripped off the smudged blouse and, wincing, stepped out of the wrinkled navy skirt. She'd had to ease gingerly into her car and the drive home had been torture. Every movement involving her tailbone was a symphony in pain.

She wondered if she should go to the minor emergency room to check if she'd cracked it, but dismissed the idea.

Instead she took four ibuprofen and a quick hot shower before redressing for the office. It was late in the afternoon, and she didn't *have* to go back, but she was always conscious of image, and she didn't want anyone to think that she'd played hooky.

Now in a black skirt and similar blouse in taupe, she forced her feet into heels, grabbed her bag and slowly made the trek out to her car, moving like the Hunchback of Notre Dame.

Agony as she got in. She prayed for the ibuprofen to work fast. And then she put the car and her dignity into gear and drove back to work.

Kylie hobbled through the glass doors of Sol Trust's building and through the tiled lobby with its jungle of tropical plants. She hoped to get to the elevator and then her office without anyone commenting, but no such luck.

To her consternation, Milty Goldman stood in the direct path of the elevators, surrounded by a group of dark-suited men whose demeanor screamed investment banker. She offered a weak smile and tried to dodge around them.

"Miss Kent," Milty boomed.

Her spine snapped to attention, causing her tailbone to shriek in pain. For a moment she couldn't move, couldn't breathe. She erased Edvard Munch's *The Scream* from her face and slowly turned around, producing her best corporate smile.

"Yes, Mr. Goldman? How are you today?" She forced one foot in front of the other in a sort of military goose step until she got to the edge of the group. She must have looked like a flamingo on Xanax.

"Kenny, Mort, Dave, Steven, I'd like you to meet Ms. Kylie Kent, one of our up-and-coming account managers, here at Sol Trust. Kylie, these gentlemen are going to give us more money to look after." He turned to them with an ingratiating smile. "Aren't you, boys?"

They all chuckled and backslapped him. Everyone was a little too jovial, and she wondered if they'd had drinks at lunch.

She kept her eyes on their faces, even though every single one of the men covertly assessed her breasts. The one called Mort openly checked out her ass.

"Will you be joining us for dinner this evening, Miss Kent?" asked Dave.

Her gaze flew to Milty's. "Oh, no, I don't think so—"

"That's a great idea, Dave," said Milty.

Worse and worse. This was clearly a case of invite-the-pretty-girl-along to keep the big boys happy, which could be very good for her career, even though it made her angry that the gesture had to do with her looks and not her competence.

She should go.

On the other hand, she couldn't possibly tolerate the agony of having to sit in a straight-backed chair in some formal restaurant for hours. She simply couldn't do it.

"I'd love to, Milty, but I took a bad fall earlier today at a customer's business and I've hurt my, er, back. My, ah, tailbone." She felt her cheeks growing warm for the second—third?—time that day.

Now all the men had an excuse to look at her backside, and they did.

Kylie gritted her teeth.

"I see," the chairman said, with an odd expression. She was clearly the only employee who'd ever turned down an invitation from him. She should probably map the way to the unemployment office on Google when she returned to her desk.

"Well, I'm sorry to hear that. I must say that your gait did seem a bit unusual."

Great. So she *had* looked like some strange bird. And now they were all checking out her legs.

Then Milty frowned. "You fell at a customer's business, you say?"

She could see him adding up nasty worker's compensation figures in his head. "Yes, but it's nothing, really. I just need to rest for a few hours this evening."

The man called Kenny clucked his tongue and rocked back

on his heels. "Can't be suing a customer for damages, now can you? Bad PR."

The other men laughed. It wasn't that funny. She decided that they had definitely been drinking.

"Oh, no! I'd never—" Kylie blanched at the idea of explaining in court documents how she'd fallen out of a walk-in fridge in a disheveled state, with the client on top of her. No, not even for fifty million dollars would she sue. Not for a hundred million.

She chuckled right along with the rest of them.

"Well," Milty said, "you boys ready for a tour of the premises?"

They all moved as a group into the reception area, and Kylie figured she'd dodged a bullet. She breathed a sigh of relief.

"Oh, Kylie," called April, the receptionist. "You have a package. Courier-delivered."

Kylie took it with thanks. The parcel was about the size of a pizza box and the wrapping was professional. "Who's it from? Was there a card?"

April shook her head.

"Must be your birthday, Miss Kent," said the tall, gangly banker named Mort.

"Happy birthday!" said the one named Steven. A chorus of happy birthdays sounded.

Kylie flushed. "It's not my—"

"Well, aren't you going to open it?" prodded Kenny.

Milty inclined his head, the king ordering his subject to comply.

"Um, sure." Kylie slid her index finger under the tape sealing the gift—if that's what it was. Probably a calendar from someone she did business with.

She unwrapped the paper and lifted the lid of the box.

All of the bankers, including Milty, craned their necks to

see the contents, and one by one they snorted with amusement at her expense.

Inside was an inflatable, red rubber doughnut for sitting on. It had been sent from a medical supply store.

And she knew exactly who it was from.

MORTIFICATION PREVENTED KYLIE from using the rubber ring at work, and the obnoxious bankers had, thank God, stopped short of suggesting that she put her lips to the inflation device and blow it up while they watched. She spent the remaining hour of the afternoon torn between outrage at Dev for sending it, helpless amusement at her own expense and fear for the repercussions to her career.

There was the silly part of her that was touched by Dev's thoughtfulness: he hadn't sent the doughnut entirely out of a desire to embarrass her. He'd actually thought she might need it.

Truth to tell, she did. But she'd rather be battered, deep-fried and served with coleslaw than have anyone she worked with see her sitting on the thing.

Kylie sat with another rapidly cooling café con leche, ostensibly running numbers on another loan, but actually agonizing over what damage she might have caused to her career today.

She'd lost her mind and her dignity in that walk-in fridge, and then turned down a dinner invitation from the CEO of Sol Trust before losing her dignity for the second time—and in front of the man who held her career in his manicured hands.

She told herself she could have made it through the evening. She could have scored some sedatives two blocks away from the bank—this was Miami, after all, capitol city of pain clinics and auto insurance fraud. A wad of cash and you could find a crooked M.D. to write a prescription for anything.

Right. Go to dinner with Milty Goldman and a bunch of

financial players stoned out of her gourd and slurring her speech? Great idea.

No telling what was actually in the meds on the street. She might not feel the pain in her tailbone, but she probably wouldn't be able to feel her own feet, either.

Kylie reminded herself that she hadn't gotten where she was in her job already by being stupid. Well, except for today.

But she continued to agonize about the repercussions. And then there was Devon and the unwelcome effect he had on her. What the hell? The guy made her drunk or something.

He was jeopardizing not only her dignity and her job, but also her self-respect. And hadn't she learned her lesson from the first dirtbag? She needed to trade up, not down, from Jack.

Jack had at least had a bright future at one point. He'd had an MBA and a vision of success, like her.

And Dev? He had a wild past, an irresponsible streak a mile wide and a dubious future as a bar owner and restaurateur. Most restaurants went belly-up within the first year of opening. She wasn't aware that he had any prior experience even managing a fast-food joint.

The more she thought about it, the more she wondered how Dev had gotten Priscilla to sign off on his business loan. There had to be a personal connection somewhere. Kylie blanched, horrified, at the thought that maybe Dev had put his charm to work on her boss in the exact same way he was applying it to Kylie herself. Had Priscilla been in the walk-in fridge?

Dear God.

When she began to wonder if her boss's baby was, in fact, Devon's, she stood abruptly, winced at the pain in her tailbone and fled the office in search of a cold glass of wine—or maybe three.

15

SATURDAY MORNING, THE Dawn of the Date, was a rough one for Dev. He'd been at the bar until 3:00 a.m. managing things. The *things* had included a spat between Marla and Maurizio, who'd underbaked a batch of potato skins then burned the replacement batch to a crisp, resulting in unhappy customers who'd bitched her out, demanded their drinks for free and left her no tip.

The *things* also included Dev having to bounce out a drunk who'd reached across the bar and honked Lila's breast like an old-fashioned bicycle horn. Lila, who'd been filling a glass with tonic at the time, turned the tonic dispenser on the guy with one hand and slapped him silly with the other.

Most normal people would have vamoosed at the time the enraged Lila started screaming Spanish invective, but this particular man stayed around to enjoy it. He then begged Lila to come home with him and spank him.

That was the point at which Dev had locked an arm around his neck, yanked him off his stool and propelled him by the belt to the exit, inviting him to come back and apologize when he was sober.

Dev himself hustled drinks until Lila came out of her subsequent snit in the ladies' room, her talons smelling of fresh nail polish.

The last *thing* he'd had to deal with before closing time was the fact that the men's room door had been locked for a solid hour and nobody could get in. Of course it fell to Dev to pound on the door and then use a master key to unlock it with great trepidation when he got no response.

This was South Beach, and literally anything could be going on in there: a long cell-phone conversation, a three-way or an overdose.

Thank God he found only one body and it wasn't dead, merely a drunk who'd passed out on the crapper. Dev threw a glass of cold water in the guy's face, turned his head while he pulled up the man's pants and then had the dubious honor of flushing before he staggered out of Bikini.

Dev used up half a can of Lysol in the room and then advised the gentleman who was waiting to use the facilities that he might wish to wait until the air freshener had taken effect before going in.

This was his glamorous life as an entrepreneur. Dev longingly eyed the full complement of rum behind the bar, but told himself to forget about it. He had to be responsible and he couldn't manage a business half in the bag.

By the time he fell into an exhausted sleep, it was almost 5:00 a.m. He woke at noon, showered and then took a look around his condo, which was a bachelor's disaster of epic proportions. Normally this wouldn't have bothered him, but since this was the Dawn of the Date, it was very possible that he'd be bringing Kylie back here for dessert.

And if he hoped to convince her that he was a good candidate for a relationship, he'd better get busy, since the girl he'd hired to clean "regularly" had been a lot less than regular lately.

Dev grimaced. This, after he'd fallen for her hard-luck

story about getting evicted from her boyfriend's apartment and given her an advance on the next three months' cleaning so she could get her own place. He hadn't seen her, of course, since he'd handed her the cash. He was a chump. Why did he have such bad luck with employees? Why was he forever giving people a second or a third chance?

But he didn't have a lot of time to think about it. First he attacked his bathroom, which would have frightened a wild hog. It took a razor to remove the scum lining the bathtub, and the toilet had become a fetid swamp. He poured an entire cup of bleach into it and flattened every bristle of the long-handled brush to get it clean. The sink was a minefield of toothpaste globs, but by the time he was done, it sparkled like new.

Every dish that he owned was crusted over with food and stacked on the counter next to the kitchen sink or in the basin itself. The dishwasher was malfunctioning, and he hadn't gotten around to doing anything about it.

Dev carried every pot, pan, utensil, cup, plate and bowl into the guest bathroom, where he placed them in the freshly sterilized bathtub and drowned them in hot water to soak. He added a quarter cup of dish detergent and stirred it around with a slotted spoon.

While the dishes sat in the hot water, he raked up all the flotsam in the living room, dispensed with most of it, then folded the armchair full of laundry for the first time since he could remember. He usually dumped the contents of the dryer into it and pulled items from the pile as needed.

He dusted then wiped the windows with glass cleaner. He threw out the petrified husk of the plant he'd managed to kill. Finally, he located the vacuum in the guest-room closet and sucked up a couple of month's worth of grunge and dust bunnies from the carpet and tile.

Dev felt pretty pleased with himself as he took inventory of the room, until he got to the grimy—and empty—fish tank.

Good luck keeping that fish alive—little boy. Kylie's words came back to haunt him.

Shit. He had to acquire another fish before tonight. Dev looked at his watch: it was already 4:00 p.m. and he'd told her he'd pick her up at seven.

He launched himself at the small tank and carried the whole thing over to the sink he'd just scrubbed. He pulled out the treasure chest, the fake plants and the reef, making a mess of the formerly pristine countertop. Dev cursed, but it couldn't be helped. He poured the dirty water down the sink, blocking the colored rocks at the bottom with his hand. The stench was awful.

Dev scooped out the rocks and rinsed them in his colander. For the next twenty minutes, he worked at removing all of the green scum, slime and algae from the walls of the tank. He went through an entire roll of paper towels and all of what was left of the glass cleaner.

Then he reassembled everything and filled the tank with water from the tap. He checked his watch. It was now almost five. He had just enough time to get to the pet store, purchase a new fish, get back with it, shower and change, and then go pick up Kylie.

Dev sprinted to the Corvette and peeled rubber out of the parking lot. The Saturday afternoon traffic was heavy and it took him a good twenty minutes to get to the pet store. He skidded in, made tracks for the fish section and chose a fish within two minutes. But the gangly teenaged salesperson— fish monger?—was absorbed in helping a mom and her tubby kid choose just the right combination of fish for *his* tank.

Dev tapped his toe and looked at his watch repeatedly as fifteen more minutes went by. Finally he asked the teenager if he could self-serve a fish. All three of them swung around and stared at him as if he'd asked to disembowel them.

Well, *excuuuuuse* him. "Sorry," he mumbled, "but I have a thing."

"I will be right with you, sir," the teenager said in disdainful tones. "As soon as I've helped these customers."

Dev cooled his heels for another ten minutes, before the boy deigned to wait on him. But the fish he'd chosen was a slick, smart little bastard, and the teenager couldn't seem to catch him with the little net he had.

Finally, Dev said, "Grab the first one you can and bag him for me." He bounced on the balls of his toes in impatience. Teen Boy finally caught one, a plump, ugly, mostly white little bugger with irregular dots of orange and bulging, accusatory eyes.

Dev dashed with him to the cash register, paid with a ten and told the cashier to keep the change. He shot outside and into the 'Vette, tossing the bagged fish onto the passenger seat. A turn of the key and a roar of the engine later, he was back in the heavy traffic.

Stop, go. Stop, go. Stop, go. Dev swerved around a PT Cruiser and cut in front of an Audi. He sped up to catch the tail end of a yellow light, and saw the cop across the intersection at the last minute. He stomped on the brakes, and the fish went flying off the seat and *splat!* Into the windshield.

The bag broke on impact, sending water pouring out.

Shit! Shit! Shit! Dev grabbed for the remnants of the bag and the fish, but the bag was a lost cause. The poor creature flipped and flopped in his hand while he looked wildly around for something to put it in. He grabbed a paper coffee cup from the console between the seats and dropped the fish into it.

But he needed some water for it immediately. The half bottle of Coke in the console would kill it. He knew there was a convenience store a couple of blocks up where he could get a bottle of water, but he didn't know if the fish could make it for more than a minute.

The light turned green.

Dev made an executive decision. He spit on the fish, set the coffee cup in the round holder in the console and hit the gas. Approximately three minutes later, he was inside the store, grabbing a bottle, unscrewing the cap and pouring water over his new buddy.

The fish lay motionless on its side for a long moment, then flopped feebly. Dev cheered and the two other customers in the store edged away from him.

Four minutes later he was in the car, headed home. The time: 6:15 p.m. He was at the condo by 6:27 p.m. and the fish was in the tank by 6:28 p.m. Dev shed his clothes and leaped into the shower at 6:29, was out and wrapped in a towel by 6:34 and fully clothed, combed and cologned by 6:41.

By 6:43 p.m. he was back in the Corvette and he pulled into Kylie's complex on the dot of seven.

She lived in a white stucco building with large semicircular balconies on the upper floors. Dev made his way inside and stood in front of the door for a moment, feeling like a thirteen-year-old asking his first girl to a PG movie. Why? He'd never had trouble picking up women. He usually delivered some outrageous line that had them either laughing or slapping his face and walking away—but usually the former. And once they were laughing, he had them in the palm of his hand.

Yeah. He, Dev, was a sex god.

So he knocked on the door.

"Hello, Dev," Kylie said as she opened it, and pulled the rubber doughnut he'd sent over his head so that it hung around his neck.

He blinked and gazed down at it. Then up at her.

Black. She wore black from head to toe, instead of white and navy. A black halter dress with black strappy heels, and vast expanses of tanned, sexy skin in between. Her blond hair tumbled over her nude shoulders, her mouth was pale and shiny and her eyes hugely dark and mysterious, thanks to more eye makeup than she usually wore. She looked like some Hollywood star in a film still.

Dev stood there with the ring around his neck and drank her in. He gawked like a tourist at the zoo.

Kylie raised her eyebrows. "Is something wrong?"

He slowly shook his head.

"Alligator got your tongue?"

He nodded.

She smiled. "Well, that's a refreshing change."

"Uh. Out of curiosity, why am I wearing this doughnut? Please tell me you don't expect me to wear it to the Rusty Pelican?"

"Is that any more embarrassing than sending it to me at work?"

Damn. His cute little gesture had backfired. "Oh. Uh. Sorry. I'm a guy. We're practical jokers, you know? We don't think a whole lot about dignity."

"I figured that out the hard way."

Uh-oh. "I thought it would make you laugh, but I also thought it might come in handy, especially that particular afternoon."

"It was a very thoughtful gift, Dev. Thank you. It just would have been better if I hadn't opened it in front of the CEO of Sol Trust and a bunch of investment bankers."

"Yikes." It was all he could think of to say.

She shrugged, then seemed to forgive him. She lifted the ring off, then tossed it onto a chair. "Yes, I did use it—but not until I got home." She rubbed at her tailbone ruefully.

"So, you feeling better?"

She nodded. "I'm fine, now, but I was pretty sore for a few days."

Dev wondered why she was still blocking her doorway and

hadn't asked him inside. "Glad to hear it. Uh, that you're fine now."

She nodded. Then she began to fidget, which seemed unlike her.

"What?" Dev asked. "Is there something wrong?"

Kylie took a deep breath. "Before I go anywhere with you, Dev, I have to ask you a question. Did you sleep with my boss to get your loan?"

16

"WHAT?" DEVON CROAKED. "No!"

Kylie seemed to sag with relief. "Oh, thank God."

"What kind of question is that?" He was outraged.

"First, let me say I'm sorry for asking it—"

"Well, you should be!" Dev almost turned around and left.

"I apologize. I really do. It's just that I was reviewing your file again, and you don't even have restaurant experience, and… Well, you're very flirtatious and, uh, you were very hard to…resist…in the refrigerator, I mean, and—"

He stared at her and shook his head. "So you thought I'd seduced your boss to get a business loan. Wow. What a compliment. I think I'm leaving, now."

"Devon, don't go." Her face was drawn in remorse, her eyes sincere, her hand outstretched.

"I may have very few morals," he said with dignity, "but I do have a *couple* left."

"Look, I'm sorry. I just had to know."

"Well, now you do."

"Can you understand that I wouldn't want to set myself up for more bad experiences after my last relationship?"

"Yeah, Kylie. I get that. But at a certain point, your suspicions turn into flat-out paranoia. I am who I appear to be, plain and simple. I've never seen your boss, your mother, your grandmother or your cat naked. Christ!"

She laughed. "How did you know I have a cat?"

"Lucky guess." He narrowed his eyes on her, feeling his mouth quirk upward and not sure how he felt about it. He was still offended.

"Well, speaking of the cat…" She tugged him inside. "Come in while I feed him and get my purse. I doubt he'll take off his fur coat for you, though." She winked.

Even though she was trying way too hard to make everything okay again, he followed her in. "I guarantee you he's not my type, anyway."

Her condo was large and airy, decorated in mostly beige and white, with touches of soft green here and there. The colors seemed to echo Kylie herself, with her blond hair and tanned skin. A rattan sofa, love seat and chair with cream cushions sat grouped around an area rug with a pattern of palm trees. A large painting on the wall over the sofa depicted a beach scene. Shells and candles were grouped on the glass coffee table. The whole effect was restful and serene.

The cat, on the other hand, eyed him suspiciously. It was a fat, cross-eyed Siamese and it hissed at him as he followed Kylie into the kitchen.

"Sorry," she said. "Potsy is very protective of his food."

"Ah." *Potsy?* "It's okay, little guy," Dev crooned. "I've never been a fan of—" he eyed the tiny can on the countertop, "—Fancy Feast. Especially not the seafood flavor."

Potsy twitched his tail, cocked his head and emitted the classic demented Siamese yowl while Kylie popped open the can and noxious fumes wafted through the air.

Dev gagged, but Potsy twitched his tail and wove manically around Kylie's legs while she scooped his foul-smelling dinner into a kitty dish.

Dev took full advantage and checked out her ass as she bent

down. His ire died a little in favor of lust. He was suddenly back to wanting to weave around her legs, too, but it was for entirely different reasons than the cat's.

He bent to pet Potsy, but the animal jumped at his touch, turned on him and snarled. Like owner, like pet. Aaargh.

He snapped upright again. "*Okay.* Maybe you'd like my fish better than you like me, huh, dude?"

Kylie shot him an apologetic glance. "Potsy's a little temperamental."

"You don't say."

"How *is* your fish, by the way?" The corner of her lovely mouth quirked.

Dev shoved his hands into his pockets and rocked back on his heels. "He's great."

"Does he have a name?"

"Uh…yes. Yes, he does." Dev wracked his brain.

She set the cat's bowl down and turned to look at him expectantly, stroking Potsy's head while he gobbled.

"Fugly. His name is, uh, Fugly."

Her expression quizzical, Kylie stood and walked to the sink to wash the fork she'd used in the cat food. "What kind of a name is that?"

As if it was any worse than Potsy? And didn't logic dictate that Potsy should be an orange cat, if the name came from the old *Happy Days* show? Oh, wait—that was Ralph Malph. Potsy had dark hair.

Dev realized that Kylie was waiting for a response. "Well, my fish is a little homely. He's a goldfish, but he's not really gold. He's dirty white, with orange speckles. And his eyes look like they're about to pop out of his head."

"Aw. He sounds cute."

Dev shrugged in discomfort, thinking of the traumas and indignities Fugly had suffered today. He changed the subject as she messed around some more in the kitchen.

Finally, she picked up her evening bag from the small dining table. "Ready to go?"

Hell, yes.

Dev was ready to go in more ways than one.

THE RUSTY PELICAN WAS a great place for sunset drinks. Set right on the water, it offered a beautiful view of Biscayne Bay and a rustic, casual atmosphere.

Kylie had been there before, but it had been a while, and she'd certainly never zoomed up to it in a chili-pepper-red Corvette with a local celebrity. Dev knew the guy at the door and the bartender, as well as the pretty waitress who led them outside to a table next to the bay. She lit a citronella candle to keep the worst of the mosquitoes away.

Kylie ordered a glass of sauvignon blanc, and Dev a Dos Equis. He lounged back in his chair and crossed his legs at the ankles, raising the beer casually in a toast. "To our first date."

She laughed self-consciously. "To our first date." Again, she wasn't sure she cared for the implication that there would be a second one. She took a sip from her glass after raising it.

The wine was cool and light, the way she wanted to keep the atmosphere between the two of them. But the sight of Dev had made her stomach do funny things, and the way he looked at her—as if he wanted to consume her whole—paradoxically raised both her body temperature and the tiny hairs at her nape that warned of danger.

Jack had never raised the hair on her neck for any reason, good or bad.

The sensual curve of Dev's lips, the aquiline nose, the tough jaw and the mirrored sunglasses all combined to make him look like some South American dictator with an army at his beck and call. Sleek, unpredictable and powerful.

"See something you like?" he asked provocatively.

How did he make her blush like a teenager? It was very annoying. Jack had never made her blush, either. "Yes," she said. "The sunset is beautiful."

His lips twitched.

But it was true. The sky was lit with a lovely neon pink that trailed papaya orange and flirted with gold streaks. Here and there white clouds scudded across the horizon, filling with pink and gold as the breeze blew them east.

"So," Dev said. "You're gorgeous and the sexiest woman I've ever seen. You were recently engaged to an idiot, and you work at Sol Trust. What else should I know about you, other than the weird fact that you're my friend's aunt?"

Kylie smiled. "You should know that I really do need to see more of your business than—" she looked toward the bay again "—the, um, refrigerator." Her blush intensified, heat pulsing in her cheeks as she recalled that day.

"Understood. You should be my date to the grand opening of the restaurant this coming Saturday. How's that?"

"Shouldn't we see how *this* date goes before planning another one?"

"This date," he said with a confidence that both amused and touched her, "is going to be the best of your life."

"It is?"

"Yes."

"Okay. I'll give you the benefit of the doubt."

"But you have to tell me who the real Kylie is."

She took another sip of wine. "What do you want to know?"

"Brothers or sisters?" Dev prompted.

"Well, my older sister is Mark's mother." She drew in a breath. "And I had an older brother. He...died."

Dev's grin vanished. "I'm sorry."

"No, it's okay. I wasn't even born yet. He was twelve, he got off the school bus. Ran around the back of it to cross the street, didn't look carefully, and a van hit him. He was killed instantly."

"That's awful."

"Yes, it was. The driver wasn't paying attention—she'd dropped something on the floor and was reaching for it. She was an out-of-towner who didn't see the stop sign around the curve in the road. Poor woman. My sister said she was absolutely hysterical."

Kylie drank more of her wine. "My parents never really got over it. Apparently my dad was a zombie for two years. My mom was a wreck. They almost split up. In fact they did separate, but somehow I came along—surprise!—and they patched things up, I guess for my sake. That's what my sister thinks, anyway. Obviously I was too young to remember."

"Were they at the wedding?" Dev asked.

"No. You have to understand, my mom was forty-six when she had me, and my dad was forty-nine. They're gone now. She died of ovarian cancer when I was nineteen and he of a heart attack a year later."

Dev leaned forward and covered her hand. "I'm sorry," he said again, clearly feeling awkward. "I didn't know."

"How could you?" Kylie traced a finger through the condensation on her wineglass, which clung to the surface like tears. She didn't want to think about the long, terrible weeks her mother had spent in the hospital, the radiation treatments, the chemo, the pain and the nausea. The scarves Kylie had made for her to cover her hair loss. Her dad's bewilderment when the doctors said there was nothing further that they could do.

He'd been blank and robotic for the year after her death. He'd done nothing but stare vacantly at the television or read the paper. Until one morning while walking down the driveway to get it, he'd dropped in his tracks.

She'd been afraid to love anyone after that, for fear that they might die on her, too. Truth to tell, she was still careful. She didn't get attached easily, and when she did, it was a calculated process. When she'd met Jack, she'd tabulated all kinds of things about him over the year that they'd dated before becoming engaged. He was athletic. He didn't smoke. He was basically a healthy eater. He didn't take unnecessary risks. He even drove a safe car....

Dev squeezed her hand, bringing her back to the present, the stunning sunset over the water and his warm, sympathetic gaze. He'd taken off the shades and tossed them onto the table. The light had gone soft and golden, and shimmered blue highlights in his hair. Gone was the South American dictator, and in his place was a dark Adonis. He was dazzling.

But this version of Dev wasn't any more trustworthy. Play with a sun god and you were pretty sure to get burned. And Dev was all about sex—even if it was real sex, not cybersex—which reminded her way too much of Jack's issues. Speaking of which, she was pretty sure she'd heard rumors that Dev drank too much. It wouldn't be surprising—the guy did own a bar. And that was definitely not a character trait she wanted in a boyfriend.

Then again, she'd picked the last one so carefully and couldn't have been more wrong about him.

"So are you close to your sister?" Dev asked.

Kylie hesitated. "Jocelyn? She's twenty-two years older than I am. We're at different stages of our lives, and always have been. But we're there for each other."

Dev nodded. "And what stage of your life are you at?"

His tone was casual, but she had the feeling that the question was very serious. "I'm focused on my career," she said firmly. "I will be a bank vice president one day."

"What about marriage? Kids?"

"If I find the right person, then I'll think about it."

Dev raised his beer to his lips and drank. "What if he's sitting right in front of you?"

He was nothing if not audacious. And persistent. She laughed softly and shook her head.

"Why is that funny? Because I don't walk around in a designer golf shirt? I'm not a member of a prestigious country club? Because I don't drive something conservative, like a BMW sedan?"

"No…"

"Let me tell you why you don't want to *meet,* much less marry, that guy." Dev had leaned forward and placed his hands flat on the table.

"Go ahead. I want to hear this."

"Yeah, you do," he said seriously. "You don't want the country club guy, because all his life, he's followed the rules. He's worn the right clothes, gone to the right school, dated the right girls. He's kissed the right asses, gotten recommendations from the right teachers, gotten the right degrees and now works at the right firm.

"Everything he does is calculated, robotically programmed for success. He sees *you,* Kylie, and what he sees is the right woman, the one he can conquer the social scene with, because you're perfect. You'll look good on his arm, you'll flatter the appropriate people and you'll have kids in his image that he can name after himself."

Dear God. He was describing Jack. Kylie swallowed more wine as Dev went on with his assessment.

"And you know what? No matter how ideal this guy looks, *he is a ticking bomb.* Why? Because he's been so busy doing everything he's supposed to do to get ahead that he doesn't even know what the hell he *wants* out of life. And when this occurs to him—and it will, because underneath it all he's a pretty smart guy—he is going to have an almighty meltdown. He's going to go off the deep end. He'll run away with a stripper, or gamble away the equity in your home, or become an alcoholic bum and sell coconuts in the islands."

Or become addicted to internet porn and pain pills after he pulls his Achilles tendon. Kylie's hands tightened unconsciously around her wineglass, transferring all the condensation to her already damp palms.

"Okay, Dev. I hear you. So what makes you the better man?"

"It's simple. I've lived a less-than-ideal life. I've been with hundreds of women—I won't lie to you. I was a man-slut, up until the very moment I saw you."

She repressed a snort at that. "Oh? And what happened in that moment?"

"Don't know," he confessed. "It was sort of mystical. I know that sounds cheesy, but my dad said the exact same thing happened to him when he met my mom."

That did something funny to her heart.

"My dad's this cynical, wickedly funny Irishman—very understated. He always thought he'd marry a strapping Irish country wench who'd beat him regularly with a rolling pin. Then he saw my Cuban mother, who is an over-the-top, still sexy, vivacious drama queen. He was a goner."

Dev winked at her.

"But I digress," he said. "Let's see. I've also done my share of illegal substances, not to mention a lot of the legal ones. I've hung out in every dive in the southeast and a bunch of others. I've lived the life I wanted to live, without asking anyone's permission or forgiveness. But I've now gotten it out of my system. Take me on today, and there won't be any surprises tomorrow." His eyes were direct and honest; his words rang true.

"*Hundreds* of women?" Kylie asked.

Dev had the grace to blush and look away. Then he recovered and shot her his signature bad-boy grin. "Well, how do you think I perfected my technique?"

She choked on her wine.

"I've been trained by all of them to do one thing—make you happy. And I haven't heard you complain yet."

Kylie's mouth hung open at his sheer outrageousness.

His eyes twinkled.

Finally, she couldn't help but laugh. "You—I don't know how you do it."

"What?"

"Take a background as a degenerate and turn it into the perfect résumé for monogamy!"

"Ah-ha. So you're seriously considering my application."

"I didn't say that." But she laughed again.

"But you are."

Thank God the waitress approached at that moment and asked if they'd like another round. They said yes, Kylie because she had a feeling she was going to need alcohol in order to deal with Dev's peculiar logic and persuasive tongue. Then again, maybe she should abstain.

She didn't.

"So how am I doing?" Dev asked.

"I don't know how to take you," Kylie admitted honestly.

"As is. On sale, especially for you."

"As is? Does that mean you come with an STD or something?"

Dev's eyebrows shot up. "As a matter of fact, I'm clean. If you want to see my medical chart, I'll have the doc fax you a copy. I may have been a slut, but I was a smart slut. I always took precautions."

"So there are no little Devon McKees running around out there?"

"Not a one." Dev looked a little regretful about that, which made her nervous. "Any further questions?"

"Any other confessions?"

His face became very serious, his mouth flattening into one thin line. "I'm afraid so."

The waitress returned with their second round and Dev remained somber.

Kylie couldn't think what he had to tell her that might be worse than what he already had. There were really only a few possibilities: he was gay. She dismissed that one. Or he'd been a drug dealer. Or he'd murdered someone.

She waited until the waitress had disappeared, but then she had to know. "Well? Dev, what is it that you have to tell me?"

"Yeah, I don't know that I can trust you with this one, Kylie."

Dread blossomed in her stomach, then dissipated as she reminded herself that she wasn't going to date this guy anyway. But—

"Devon, you're scaring me. Do you dismember people for fun?"

"Nah. Too messy."

She cast about for other grisly possibilities. "You're a contract killer?"

He shook his head, still looking grave despite his flip response earlier.

"You're a spook? An international arms dealer? A—?" She swallowed hard as the worst thing possible came to mind. "You're not a pedophile?"

His jaw dropped open. *"No."*

"Then what is it you have to tell me?" Her voice had risen to almost a shriek.

"Patience is a virtue, Kylie."

"I'm fresh out! Tell me, for the love of God."

He heaved a deep sigh. "Well, okay. I guess I'll have to."

17

DEV GAZED INTO HER EYES and took her hands in his. He could
see the doubt growing in her eyes and feel the tension in her
fingers as they lay in his.

"I'm hungry," he said.

She stared at him. "That's it? That's your big confession?"

He nodded.

"You— You—" She tried to pull her hands away but he
held on tight.

Dev laughed as she smoldered across the table.

"I thought you were going to tell me that you'd murdered
someone."

"Would you like me to?"

"No."

"Dry-cleaner didn't press your suit well? Fast-food worker
gave you the wrong order? Bag boy at the grocery store squish
your bread? I'll do away with 'em and toss 'em in the bay."

"McKee, you are so obnoxious." She gave a final tug and
got one hand back, which she put immediately on her wineglass and brought it to her lips.

"It's an appealing quality in a man, I think," he mused,
draining half of his beer.

"Appalling is more like it."

He grinned in appreciation. "So, I have no more terrible secrets to tell you. They're all on the table."

"No skeletons still in the closet? You're sure?"

"My skeletons are way too shameless to stay in the closet. They dance around in public with a microphone, just like I did. Now, how about you?"

"What about me?"

"Have you ever done anything bad? Or are you as good as you look?"

Kylie repressed a smile, causing a dimple to appear at the corner of her mouth.

"Uh-huh. I thought so. What was it?"

She caught her lower lip between her teeth and looked up at him from beneath her lashes. "I set my fiancé's laptop on fire."

"You *what?*" Dev burst out laughing.

"He— Well, he liked to look at porn on the web. A lot. He got obsessed with it. And he'd drink and pop pills. So one day I came home and found him passed out in our bed with his laptop. And I don't need to tell you what was on it. That day was *it* for me. I had reached the breaking point. So I took the laptop out to the barbecue grill, lined it with foil and set the laptop inside. Then I turned on the gas and lit it."

"You lined the grill with foil, first," Dev repeated, in disbelief.

"Yes. I didn't want to ruin the grill, just the computer."

He shook his head, his mouth working.

"Then I went inside and packed all my stuff and got a friend to come help me move it out. Jack never woke up once. He was out for hours, oblivious."

"You didn't have furniture there?"

She shrugged. "It wasn't nice. We were waiting to buy new stuff until after we got married."

"How recent was this, again?"

"Eight months ago."

Dev nodded. "So when he woke up, you were gone."

"Pretty much. He called me, cussing, and said I owed him an explanation and an apology. I gave him the explanation— not that I hadn't warned him many times what would happen if he didn't pull himself together—told him to get help and that *he* owed *me* the apology."

She pressed her lips together as if to keep her emotions from escaping. There were no tears in her eyes, but he could see the pain there.

"I'm guessing you never got it."

"No. And I never will."

Dev was still holding her hand in his, and he felt it quiver. He stroked the back of it with his thumb. They sat there in silence for a few moments.

Then Kylie pulled her hand away.

Dev pursed his lips. "So, tell me the truth. Did this guy wear golf shirts?"

Kylie gulped the rest of the wine while looking darkly at him over the rim of the glass. Then she nodded as she put it down. "And he drove a blue BMW sedan."

"I *knew* it." He slammed a fist onto the table.

She began to laugh. "And he was looking at country clubs to join…"

"See, you should stick with the black T-shirt kind of guy, like me." Dev nodded, poking himself in the chest with his index finger. "I rest my case."

"You've argued well, counselor," she agreed. "With somewhat skewed logic, but it works for you."

"So you'll retain me, then."

"Don't push it. Take me to dinner and keep talking."

So Dev did. He took her to the Ritz-Carlton on Lincoln Road, and they ate in Bistro One LR. They shared an intimate poolside table, with romantic lighting and an infinity view of the Atlantic.

Dev watched her eat king crab with clear enjoyment of both her food and the ambience. She ate the crab delicately, as if she were afraid to hurt it, which he found amusing.

She was such a study in contradictions. A lady who'd come on to him like a whore at first meeting; a prim bank executive who'd let it all hang out at the most formal of occasions. A hard-hitter who blushed.

Kylie looked up with a mouthful of crab and caught him watching her. She finished chewing self-consciously, swallowed and dabbed at her mouth with a napkin. "What?"

He smiled. "It's about time someone treated you well. You deserve it."

"This is beautiful, Dev. Thank you."

"You're beautiful. The pleasure's all mine."

"You know, at some point we really should talk about business."

"Yeah," he agreed. "But now's not the time."

She nodded. "Fair enough. So what about your family, Dev? Did you grow up here?"

He nodded. "Like I said, my mom is Cuban, and my dad's Irish. That can be a strange combination, but their core values are the same, and they definitely gave us all a love of music. We all know how to party, too." He grinned.

"How many is *all?*"

"There are four of us—Ciara, Bettina, Aidan and me. My mom got to name the girls, and my dad named us boys. I'm the youngest."

The waiter took away the remains of their first courses. Then he brought Dev's beef brisket and Kylie's wild salmon.

"What did your parents think of their baby becoming a rock star?"

"That I'd outgrow it. They've been really supportive,

though—aside from the occasional lecture on my lifestyle. They'll be at the grand opening. You'll meet them. They'll love you."

"Oh, great," Kylie said, avoiding his gaze.

Clearly she didn't feel that they were at the meeting-his-parents stage yet. Dev resolved to change that as soon as possible.

"Yeah, they'll be so shocked to meet a nice girl on my arm that they'll have you fitted for a wedding gown on the spot," he joked.

"Ha," said Kylie faintly. "*Fantastic* salmon." She reached for her wine again.

"Glad you like it," Dev said. He couldn't resist torturing her a little. "So, do you cook?"

"Me? No."

"Ah, that's okay. Mom will give you copies of all her good Cuban cookbooks. You'll have to learn Spanish, of course, to read them, but you'll pick it up fast."

"Uh—"

"You like plantains?"

"Not exactly…"

"You should definitely develop a taste for them, because—"

"Wait a minute, Dev, hold on." Kylie set down her fork. "Just because I went out on a date with you, doesn't mean that— I mean, I'm not going to *marry* you!"

He produced his most wounded expression. "You could at least wait until I ask before you turn me down."

"I— But—"

"Relax, Kylie. I'm only teasing you."

She breathed a sigh of relief but then she got that look in her eye again. The look that said she was going to kill him with her bare hands. It was very entertaining.

Dev forked some brisket into his mouth and smiled at her while he savored it. It was tender, smoky, tangy and delicious.

He wondered if he could smuggle some to Bodvar to see if he could reproduce it. Then he dismissed the thought. Bodvar would probably throw a Nordic tantrum and quit if Dev even asked him to taste the food from another restaurant, much less food from the Ritz.

"Dev, how did you end up becoming a rock star?"

He laughed. The term sounded so cheesy. "I never was a star."

"You were—still are—pretty well-known, though."

"Only around here. We played at clubs and charity events and some weddings and bar mitzvahs. Kylie, we started in my garage, for Christ's sake. I went on to study music, and I eventually hooked up with some guys who were better than my high school buddies, but it's not like I was Tommy Lee or Jon Bon Jovi or anything. We never had a national following."

"Did you record any albums?"

"Yeah. We had three different CDs out. But again, without a big label behind you, you're not going to make much of a splash. We had some articles done on us in the Miami papers, and even as far north as Orlando, but…" He shrugged.

"You have to play one of the CDs for me," she said. "I want to hear you."

"Okay. Later."

"So when did you decide to walk away from it and open Bikini?"

Dev's chest tightened, and he felt the familiar dark weight of guilt and depression settle around his heart. He felt tired and gray whenever he thought about Wilbo. "We lost a guy," he said. It sounded stupid to his own ears. As if they'd misplaced him. "A good friend. My oldest friend."

Across the table, Kylie swallowed and put down her fork. "Lost him?"

"He died of an overdose," Dev said shortly. "Right in front

of me. Yeah, I know—how clichéd can you get? A rock musician ODs. It's such an old story that it creaks when you tell it."

"It's not a cliché when it's a dear friend of yours," Kylie said. She touched her fingers to his. "I'm so sorry."

"Thanks." Dev put another forkful of brisket into his mouth, but it could have been a tofurkey for all he cared.

"What was his name?"

"Will. We used to call him Wilbo. He played bass guitar. We went to grade school together." Wilbo, with his big ears and pointy chin…he'd looked like a demented little elf. Of course, Dev had looked like a giraffe in those days.

"We learned the multiplication tables right next to each other, and long division, too. In Mrs. Clark's class." His mouth twisted. "We read all the Encyclopedia Brown books, the Lloyd Alexander books and then the C. S. Lewis ones. We'd pretend we were the characters in them." A lump grew in his throat, and he tried to ignore it.

"We learned how to play guitar together. Started a garage band. He loved Rush and Talking Heads and—" He broke off before he broke down.

"You miss him." She said it as a statement, not a question.

Dev pushed his plate away. "Yeah. I miss him."

She continued to look at him, her gaze unwavering, a question in them.

"I wish that instead of partying right along with him, I'd dragged his ass to rehab. I wish I hadn't made him play the night he died, but I did. I wanted this record producer to notice us." Dev cracked his neck, and then his knuckles, right at the table—even though it was guaranteed not to impress Kylie. "He might be alive today if I hadn't pushed him on stage that night to perform."

She squeezed his fingers, and he looked down, vaguely surprised.

"You can't blame yourself for what happened, Dev."

"Why not? His parents do. To this day, they won't even speak to me. I'm the one who brought him into the band. I'm the one who got the gigs, created the lifestyle that killed him."

"That's not fair. You're not responsible for what he chose to put into his body."

Dev broke the contact and scrubbed at his face with both hands. "Maybe, maybe not. I put a lot of bad stuff into my body, too. Why am I alive, and he's not? Why was I able to walk away from it, and he wasn't?"

Kylie shook her head. "Only God knows the answers to questions like that."

Dev decided that it was time to steer the conversation away from this morbid topic. It made him want to drink. A lot. It made him want to smoke. And he didn't need to do either of those things. When he did, he ended up doing dumb things that hurt people.

"So," he said with determined cheer. "What would you like for dessert?"

Kylie looked as if she wanted to say more; wanted to keep him talking about this. But she didn't push the issue, and Dev was grateful.

He didn't talk about Will to anybody but his buddy Pete, and even that was rare.

"I don't need dessert, Dev," Kylie said.

He put the past behind him again and winked at her. "Oh, yes, sweetheart, you do. You absolutely do."

18

THEY SHARED A CHOCOLATE confection and then left for Dev's apartment. Aside from her feet hurting in the stilettos, Kylie felt loose, happy and more at ease than she'd ever remembered feeling. Dev brought out a side of her that she wasn't used to sharing. He didn't allow her to be careful, to hold back. She wasn't sure what it was about him—maybe his charm, maybe his sheer outrageousness, the way he made her laugh like a loon. Or maybe it was because Dev withheld judgment. He admitted his own foibles and past—so he was unlikely to hold hers against her.

While she and Jack had been used to each other, she'd always felt a mild, unspoken tension with him. As if there was something she should say to fill the air. Or she'd look up to find him watching her and feel lacking somehow, a little uncomfortable. She realized now that he'd probably been comparing her in his mind to one of his airbrushed beauties.

With Dev, what she saw seemed to be truly what she got. He was shameless, but the more she thought about it, the more his speech about the guy in the golf shirt made sense. Jack hadn't been in love with her. He'd simply seen her as the perfect wife, an accessory to his life.

As she and Dev sped through the streets of Miami in

the Corvette, a question rose in her mind. "Remember your speech about the guy in the golf shirt and how he only saw me in relation to him? As fitting the bill, or something. Well, how do *you* see me?"

A slow smile spread across Dev's face, and he took his time answering. In fact, he pulled into the parking lot of his complex and cut the car's engine before he did.

He turned to her and traced the outline of her lips with his index finger. "I see something wild, underneath a smooth, calm, lovely exterior. I see a troubled woman who's been hurt and taken advantage of, and who wants to choreograph and control her next relationship. She wants to be on top, in more ways than one. And that's okay. She glories in her sexuality but is afraid of it at the same time. She sees it as a weakness when it's really a strength."

Kylie could barely breathe as he continued. "I see humor, intelligence, kindness, beauty, grace and quiet ambition." Dev dropped his finger and kissed her. His lips were light, but they lingered. His touch went straight to her tummy, releasing hundreds of butterflies.

"Bottom line," said Dev, "I see you as a gift. For as long as you choose to remain in my life. And it is, very much, your choice."

A lump the size of a Volkswagen rose in her throat. Then she impaled herself on the gearshift while trying to reach him.

"Whoa," he said, laughing. "I guess that was a good answer."

"It was a *great* answer." She climbed into his lap—not that it was easy—and settled her mouth over his.

Dev was hard already. She pressed her body against him and he groaned. His hands tightened around her waist and then moved down to her hips. He moved his own urgently.

"I think it's time we got out of this car and went into my place," he said into her ear. "C'mon."

When she nodded, he opened the door, picked her up and set her on the pavement outside. Then he got out and they walked hand in hand into his building.

His place was on the twenty-first floor, with a stunning view of the bay. Dev unlocked the door, ushered her inside and immediately went to put on some music. Something soft and low-key. Some Ella Fitzgerald should do the trick. "You like old jazz?" he asked.

"Love it." She took in the view, and then his spare, modern furniture in caramel leather. He didn't have much on the walls—a few black-and-white photographs in light wood frames.

"Nice place," she murmured. "Mind if I use the bathroom?"

"Take your pick. There's one in there and one back through here. I'll get you some wine. Red or white?"

"White, please. Thanks." Kylie moved in the direction of the guest bath.

The kitchen sparkled, if he did say so himself. He got a wineglass out of a cabinet. He had to rinse it because it had been so long since it'd been used. In fact, it was probably the only clean dish he—

"Oh, *shit*. Oh, no, no, *no,*" Dev said out loud. But there was nothing he could do at this point, except brain himself with the corkscrew.

Kylie's heels clicked across the floor as he opened the wine and poured. "Dev?"

He winced before she even said anything. "Uh-huh?"

"Do you always wash your dishes in the bathtub?" The expression on her face was half horror, half amusement.

He set down the bottle. "I can explain that."

"You *can?*"

"Yes. Really."

"I'll bet this is going to be interesting." She accepted her glass with a nod of thanks.

And so, while Ella Fitzgerald sang about makin' whoopee, Dev told her about his MIA cleaning person and his broken dishwasher. "Everything sort of piled up," he finished lamely. "It all needed to soak, and I was running out of time, so I threw it all in the tub and used about half a bottle of Palmolive. Then I forgot about it."

"See, here's the thing," Kylie said, as she lounged against his kitchen counter. "If you'd pulled the shower curtain, I'd have never known."

"Yeah. Bummer on that. So...does this mean I get domestic demerits or something like that?"

She laughed. "You cleaned up this entire place for me, didn't you?"

"Kind of," he admitted.

"Well, I think that's sweet. And at least the dirty dishes weren't stuffed in the oven. They were in actual water, with soap."

"Right!" he said. "That's a definite bonus."

She winked at him, while Ella began to sing about how her heart belonged to daddy.

"Would you like to go out on the balcony?" Dev suggested, moving toward the sliding glass doors.

"Sure, as long as you don't have all your dirty laundry stashed out there." But she followed him.

"Not even a sock," he said with all the dignity he could muster.

At this time of night, the water was mostly dark, lit here and there by boats and far-off cruise ships. The humidity had dropped a little with the sun, and while it had to compete with the stiff breeze out on the balcony, it still enveloped them in its wet warmth.

Condensation appeared immediately on Kylie's glass. Dev

wasn't a big white-wine fan, so he'd grabbed a bottle of beer
He lit a candle protected by glass and brought that outside
where he set it on a small table between two cushioned lounge
chairs.

Then he moved to the railing, where she stood looking ou
at the water, and slipped an arm around her. As his skin me
hers, he felt a slow burn ignite inside him. The breeze blew he
hair against his cheek, and he inhaled the scent of her shampoo, which smelled like peaches. She wore a light floral perfume that drew his mouth to her neck, wanting to taste it. And
once he'd nibbled there, he moved to her lips, which tasted
sweetly of chocolate and wine.

He didn't think he'd ever get enough of her mouth, the secretive, feminine curves of it that promised so much and ye
hid much more than they revealed.

He delved into it, trying to solve the puzzle that was her
seeking out all the nooks and crannies and mysterious little
islands. She explored him as well, winding both arms around
his neck and threading her fingers through his hair. She kissed
him like a woman on a mission, not one submitting to a seduction.

Dev stroked the smooth, hot skin of her back, a wide swath
of flesh revealed by her halter dress. He moved his fingers
down each vertebra of her spine and lingered in the hollows
between them. He caressed her nape.

And without asking permission or forgiveness, he made
quick work of the knot behind it. Kylie's dress fell to her wais
and would have dropped to the cement floor of the balcony
except that she caught it with one hand and a gasp. "Dev!"

"It's okay," he said. "Nobody can see." Each balcony was
semiprivate, with side walls.

But she seemed concerned about the candlelight, and
people below.

He shook his head. "Believe me, I've looked up here from

down there, and the most you can see when the balcony is dark is a silhouette. That's if you're looking hard at one unit."

"But—"

He blew out the candle. "What are you worried about? A telephoto lens? Trust me. I'm not that famous. Never was." He took her beautiful face in his hands and kissed her until she seemed to forget about modesty. She lost her hold on her dress, and it dropped into a puddle around her feet.

He could feel her breasts, heavy and warm, against his chest. Dev slid his hands from her face to her shoulders, down her back and to that incredible, bare ass of hers.

She shivered with pleasure, and, he guessed, the sheer freedom of being outside on a balcony nude. He stepped back from her, holding her by the shoulders. "Just let me look at you, out here in the moonlight."

He stepped back again, until his calves hit the edge of the nearest chaise. Dev sat down and drank his fill of her with his eyes. Her long, slender legs beckoned him, and so did the prize between them. Her breasts were so perfect that they defied description. Her skin appeared luminous in the moonlight.

She looked like some kind of sex goddess, standing in front of him without shame, a half-shy, half-sly smile playing on those lips. A sort of Mona Lisa smile, except frankly Dev thought Mona was homely as hell.

It hit him now, though, that the smile she was famous for could only have been produced by one thing: the chick had been stark naked when da Vinci had painted her. The ugly black dress had been painted on later—Dev would stake his restaurant on it.

Kylie, though, was anything but homely. He started to rise so that he could lick every inch of her, but stopped, taken aback, as her stiletto appeared in the center of his chest.

She pushed him back down. "Take off your shirt, Devon," she ordered.

Well. She didn't need to ask twice. Dev peeled it up and over his head, then dropped it.

"Now your shoes, socks, pants…everything. I want you buck naked and I want you ready for me." Kylie took a sip of her wine and then ran her tongue around her lips.

Dev obeyed. Very quickly.

"Now, lie back," she said. She poured a trickle of wine down each breast and, mesmerized, he watched the rivulets run down the lovely planes and swells of her body. The liquid eventually followed gravity, some pooling in her navel and some glistening in the hair at the apex of her thighs. She parted them, and the wine trickled down farther.

Dev wanted to pull her down on top of him and take her until the moon blushed, but once again, she stopped him as he tried to get to his feet, and the spike of her heel dug into his stomach this time.

"Did I give you permission to move?"

Dev shook his head.

"Then don't." She walked forward now, all wicked curves and crevices. She trailed her fingers from his knees, up the inside of his thighs, and up to the patch of hair on his chest— brushing over his balls and his erection with the lightest of tantalizing touches.

Then she swung a leg over the chaise and stood over him, giving him cardiac arrest and an eyeful at the same time. She cupped her own breasts in her hands and then let them fall. She rubbed the tips with her palms. And she bent low over him, so that they almost touched his face. But when he tried to touch them, to sit up and kiss them, she pushed him down.

He was painfully hard, harder than titanium, and she made matters worse by rubbing her breasts against his chest, now. And then she moved back and slid lower, so that his cock was imprisoned between them. He almost came at the very sight of that.

He almost lost it again as she moved backward yet again and began to rub herself intimately on him, slick and ready and teasing.

Dev heard heartfelt curses and soft pleas coming from his own mouth. He seized her hips, intent on driving into her, but she grabbed his wrists and pulled his hands away. Then, and only then, did she lower herself onto him. One inch, maybe two. Then she lifted off again, the tease.

"Please," he begged hoarsely. "Please."

She found him again with her body, and shimmied down another couple of inches before moving up. He wanted it all. He wanted to bury himself so deeply in her that nobody would ever be able to find him again.

He felt red-hot, almost insane with wanting, with pure, raging lust. And finally, *finally!* She took him all the way inside and ground her hips into his groin.

For the third time, he almost came prematurely. But he got a grip on her hips and forced her to stay still for a long moment, then two. "Make it last," he said in a gruff voice he almost didn't recognize as his own. "It's so good. Let's make it last."

When he was past the point of immediately embarrassing himself, he let her ride him. She was heavy-lidded, hair wild, hips liquid as her body worked him for pleasure. Her lips were parted and her breath came in shallow pants that turned into little moans as she built to a crest of pleasure. She looked surprised by it as the wave crashed over her and a small, astonished cry ripped from her throat.

She trembled and shivered around him, adding to his own orgasm as he came immediately afterward, feeling as if every nerve in his body—and probably the entire world—had shot in a giant, intensely happy stream out of his dick. She collapsed forward onto his chest, their bodies slick with perspiration, still joined.

19

THEY ALMOST FELL asleep like that, Kylie straddling Dev with her cheek against his chest. But after a few minutes her legs began to cramp, and she slipped off him to grope for her dress.

Dev blinked myopically in the moonlight, his hair wild, his expression slack. "You stole my bones," he said.

Kylie chuckled. "I think the normal expression is that I jumped them."

"Ain't nothin' normal about what just happened between us." Dev shook his head and fumbled for his beer.

"It was good," Kylie said carefully.

"Good? Honey, there's a bona fide *rainbow* coming off the end of my dick."

She stumbled as she stepped into her dress. What was she supposed to say? She laughed again, weakly. "Right. I think I see a leprechaun climbing up the side of your building." She glanced away from his face and inside his apartment. "And there's a pot of gold—oh, no. It's your fish tank."

"Funny," muttered Dev, still sprawled like a naked Gumby in the chaise lounge.

"I'm, uh, going to use the facilities and then pay my respects to Fugly. Isn't that what you said his name was?"

He nodded, his face looking weirdly blank. Had she hurt his feelings somehow?

Kylie padded to the door and slid it open, then closed it behind her. The cool, dry air was a shock after the warmth and humidity of the balcony, and she shivered on her way to the bathroom.

What did Dev mean when he'd said what happened between them wasn't normal? He'd been with hundreds of women. It stood to reason that he'd had good—okay, excellent...okay, *mind-blowing*—sex before.

And as for her, yes: the sex had been amazing. But she was old enough now, mature enough, to know that a lot of that was due to novelty. And a feeling of risk or daring, since Dev didn't have a pinstriped bone in his body. He wasn't her usual type.

No matter how much he might be deluding himself at the moment that he wanted a real relationship, he'd grow bored with one very quickly. He'd grow bored of *her*. Just like Jack had.

So that was that. She might enjoy having sex with Dev, but she wasn't about to fall for him or give him any power over her emotionally. It would be stupid.

She washed her hands then pressed them against the reddened skin around her mouth where Dev's five o'clock shadow had abraded her. As for the smugly satisfied expression on her face, she avoided thinking too long about it.

She headed for the fish tank. It was small and rectangular, perched on a stand in the corner of the living room. At first, she thought that a piece of plastic was floating on the surface in the front corner. But as she got closer, she saw that it was a fish. A white, speckled, ugly fish with a large protuberant eye, lying on its side. It wasn't moving at all.

Gently she tapped the glass, but got no response. Fugly was

oblivious. It became clear to her that Fugly, in fact, had gone to the Great Fish Tank in the Sky. Poor little thing.

She turned and walked to the balcony door. She slid it open and said, "Dev? I think something's wrong with your fish."

"No!" Dev scrambled off the chair, a look of horror on his face. "No, no, no, no, no…"

She moved out of the way as he ran inside and stood naked in front of the tank, his hands on his hips. He bent forward and tapped on the glass. "Fugly? Fugly? Wake up, boy!"

His expression was truly anguished. "C'mon, buddy…don't do this." Then he hit himself in the forehead with his palm. "*Damn it!* It's all my fault. I forgot to condition the water when I—" He shot her a furtive look.

"When you what?"

"I, uh, cleaned his tank today. And changed out the water. When you do that, you have to add a conditioner to the water and wait an hour or so before you can put him back in. I was in a hurry and forgot to do that."

"Because of me?"

He shrugged, looking miserable.

"You're saying that I'm the instrument of Fugly's demise?"

"No. No, not at all." Again, he looked guilty, furtive, as if he'd been engaged in some criminal conspiracy. He dragged a hand down his face. "Poor little guy. God, I feel so bad."

Kylie put a hand on his arm. "Dev, you made a simple mistake. It was an accident."

He shook his head. "I murdered him." He walked to the kitchen, and she couldn't help admiring his buns. They were world class.

"You did not *murder* your fish," she said, trying not to laugh.

"If I hadn't been driving like a maniac—" Dev clamped his mouth shut and grabbed the bottle of wine. "Refill?"

"No, thanks. So what does driving have to do with the death of your fish?"

"Huh? Oh. Nothing. Nothing at all."

"Dev, you're not making any sense." She frowned at him.

"Forget it."

"Okay."

"Want to watch a movie?" he asked, still eyeing the dead fish with what seemed to be disproportionate emotion.

"I'd probably better get home," she said.

"You don't want to stay the night?"

"Oh. Well. Thanks, but—"

"No thanks." He looked so forlorn she almost changed her mind.

"Dev, you told me yourself that Fugly had some kind of fish flu, so—"

"Right," he said, his head swiveling toward her like a robot's. "He *did*. That's why I took him to the vet this afternoon. That's why he was in the car. And I drove fast, and his bag fell on the floorboard, which probably upset him." He said it all too fast, too conveniently. With a fixed smile.

Kylie was certain he was lying. What she didn't understand was why. "You took your fish to the vet?"

"Well, yeah. He needed a doctor."

"And what did the vet do?" She folded her arms across her chest and waited for the story to get even better. He didn't disappoint her.

"He...well, he took one look at him and said he probably had this virus that's been going around."

Right. Because people take their fish to the fish park, where they play together. Chase balls and sticks.

"And he took his temperature."

"Really. How exactly did he do that?"

"With a tiny thermometer. Right up the little guy's bung hole. Yeah. Never seen anything like it."

Kylie raised her eyebrows.

"And then he gave him a little bitty fish shot and sent us on our way."

"No pills?" She asked the question to see what he'd make up next.

"Nah. But listen, you wouldn't believe the bill—"

"No, I wouldn't," she said dryly. "Dev, how stupid do you think I am?"

"Ha!" he said, with a wary glint in his eye. "Just yanking your chain."

"No," Kylie shook her head, "I don't think you were. I think you actually expected me to believe you. What I don't get is why you'd lie to me about taking a fish to a vet."

Dev opened his mouth as if he had a reasonable answer to this question.

Kylie held up a hand. "Why don't you get dressed and you can tell me all about it on the drive to my place."

Dev wondered if it was his spit that had killed Fugly. Maybe saliva was toxic to fish. Or maybe it had been the impact with the windshield. Or the minute or two without water. And then the nonconditioned tank had finished him off. At any rate, life for Fugly had been ugly, brutish and short.

Dev asked Fugly's spirit for forgiveness as he unlocked the passenger door for Kylie, who was ominously silent and, unfortunately, fully dressed once again.

Hell. How had the perfect evening ended on such a sour note? Drinks had been great. Dinner had been fantastic. The balcony sex had been sublime. And now this.

Dev cleared his throat. "I was just kidding around with you, Kylie."

"No, you weren't. You were trying to cover up your earlier slipup about driving with the fish. Which confuses me even more."

Dev sighed. "All right, all right. Here's how it was. I got home after Mark's wedding and my fish Ike had died."

"Ike?" Kylie wrinkled her brow.

"Yes, Ike. Remember the fish flu? Well, Ike was my original fish. And you'd mocked me about— Well, you said that if I couldn't keep a goldfish alive, then it didn't bode well for me having a relationship."

"Go on," Kylie said.

"So I came home and Ike was dead. And today, in the face of the possibility that I'd be bringing you here, I decided that you couldn't see that I'd killed my fish. It was embarrassing, and it was hard not to view it as some kind of omen. So I got a replacement for him—Fugly. But I was in a hurry..." Dev told her the whole miserable story. He was immensely relieved when she laughed.

"*That's* why you told me you took him to a vet?"

"Yeah," he admitted sheepishly.

"Dev, that's the most pathetic thing I've ever heard," she said, trying to catch her breath.

"It's pretty bad," he agreed.

"And now you've killed *two* fish."

He stepped harder on the gas and took the next turn with a slight squeal. "Yeah. I'm a regular fishicidal maniac."

Except for the car's engine, silence fell in the car. "So when can I see you again?" Dev asked after a couple of moments.

She didn't reply.

Dev got a bad feeling. "Kylie?"

"You lied to me."

This was not happening. "Kylie," he said in even tones, "I fibbed about a *fish*."

"You misrepresented the facts, you lied and then you tried to cover up the lie."

"Aw, damn it!" He banged his hand on the steering wheel. "I did it for *you*."

She shook her head. "No, Dev, you did it for yourself. You didn't want to look bad in front of me."

"Okay. Fine. Guilty as charged, Your Honor. Charge me and give me probation. But don't walk away over such a little thing. That's ridiculous."

She sighed. "It's a little thing this time. But next time it might not be."

"What, you think I'll do this with a dog?"

"No."

"A woman? Kind of hard to pull off, don't you think?"

"Dev, you know what I mean. The fact that you're lying to me on a first date…what kind of lies will you tell later on?"

"None! I'd never lie about anything big." Dev swung the Corvette into her parking lot with a feeling of doom. He got out to open her door, but she didn't wait for him. She was already out of the car.

"Thank you for a really wonderful evening, Dev. I do mean that. It was close to magical." Her tone, as she said the last sentence, was full of regret. Yet he detected a strange hint of something else. What was it?

Relief. There was relief mixed in with the regret, and he caught it in her demeanor, too.

She turned and walked toward her unit without waiting for him, but he caught up easily.

"I'll see you to your door."

"It's okay, really."

"No, it's not." He matched her step for step. "I want to know you're safely inside before I leave."

"Thanks."

As they arrived at her door, he asked, "So will you still be my date for the grand opening?"

She turned to face him. "I'll go with you in a business capacity. As a representative of the bank. How's that?"

Dev tried to tamp down his frustration, but he didn't mince words. "Frankly, I think it sucks."

She winced, then looked away.

"And you know what else I think? You're using this whole damn fish thing as an excuse not to get involved with me. Because you're scared to venture out of your comfort zone. You're afraid to try something new. You're terrified of your own feelings."

"You're wrong. I don't trust you." Kylie dug her keys out of her purse.

"No, sweetheart. You don't *want* to trust me." And with that parting shot, he turned and walked away.

20

KYLIE WALKED INTO HER apartment and was greeted by an unpleasant surprise: Potsy had coughed up a giant, matted hairball in the middle of her sofa.

He came to greet her, waddling in and emitting his signature, throaty half-warble, half-croak of a meow.

She sighed. "Thank you, Potsy. It was incredibly thoughtful of you to leave me such a nice gift." She kicked off her heels and padded barefoot into the kitchen to get paper towels and stain remover.

"Why *should* I want to trust Devon McKee?" she asked the cat. "Give me one good reason. Why *would* I want to trust him? He's probably just like Jack. Maybe even worse. I've *had* it with trusting men. They aren't worthy. And if they are worthy, like my dad, then they go and *die* on you."

Potsy yowled.

She grabbed his disgusting hairball through four layers of paper towel and stomped off to drop it in the trash. Then she returned and doused the remnants with the stain remover. She glared at the mess and waited for the chemicals to sink in and do their thing.

"Where does that superior tone of Dev's come from, and that implied challenge to my judgment, when he just go through telling me a pack of lies for the dumbest reason on the planet?"

Potsy squinted at her and then licked himself in an uncouth place.

"Hey, would you cut that out?" she said. "You're going to cough up another mess."

Potsy ignored her.

"But it's your nature to lick yourself, right? Just like it's his nature to lie or cheat and it's my nature to attract these loser men." Kylie started to blot up the stain.

Potsy gnawed on something between his toes, the identity of which she didn't want to know. Ugh.

"Well, he's not a loser, exactly…but I don't know if I'd call him a winner. He seems kind of on the cusp—like he could go either way."

Potsy commenced a nasty slurping noise, between a different set of toes.

She cast him a glance of distaste and glanced at her watch. It was almost one o'clock in the morning. Too late to call a girlfriend—even Melinda.

Bad television didn't seem the answer to distract herself. She'd read all her latest paperbacks. The call of the internet held no appeal. Which left work.

She went over to her soft-sided briefcase and withdrew Dev's file to examine the numbers. Because despite the date, she was going to have to pay a professional visit this next week before the grand opening.

Kylie curled up in her favorite reading chair and delved into the figures. Dev's assets were his old SUV, the Corvette and his condo, which he'd put up as collateral for the business loan since he had very little equity in the building housing Bikini. Value of the condo had dropped by half since the big mortgage crisis had kicked in, so the restaurant's loan wasn't nearly as secure as it once had been.

She also felt that, according to the business plan he'd submitted, his cash outlay was underestimated and his revenue was overestimated. Especially since he'd hired more staff and waiters for the upcoming opening of the restaurant. And then there were the actual girls he brought in to model bikinis all night and flirt with the customers.

Kylie ran numbers on her laptop for another hour and didn't like what she saw. She didn't like it at all.

Under the loan agreement, the second installment of the loan would only be paid out pending the account manager's approval. And unless she was missing some vital information or the grand opening was a smashing success and launched celebrity patronage of the place, Kylie didn't see any way she could responsibly grant that approval to Dev.

She cursed herself for unknowingly crossing the line between professional and personal with him. And then crossing it again with full knowledge that she had a conflict of interest. Not for the first time, she wished she'd passed the account to someone else immediately when she'd found out Devon McKee was the client. But at the time, she'd been unwilling to call attention to herself, and afraid of what Dev might say to bank management in retribution. She'd been an idiot where he was concerned—and still was.

DEV DROVE TOO FAST AND too aggressively after dropping off Kylie. He headed straight for Bikini to check on things, even though he'd asked his buddy and fellow groomsman Pete to make sure the place was under control. Adam had said he'd stop by, too. Either one of them could talk Lila off the ledge as well as Dev could, and easygoing Pete was a natural with the rest of the staff, too. He was the ultimate people-person and customer-service guy.

Dev squealed into the tiny lot near the bar and saw Pete's car there, thank God. He stalked towards Bikini.

How could Kylie peg him as a liar just because he'd told fish fibs? For that she found him untrustworthy? Ridiculous.

But they were *lies,* said his conscience, unaccountably not in its normal coma.

Dev scoffed. A whitewash story didn't count as a lie.

Yes it does.

Okay, fine. But it was harmless.

Evidently not, dude. She's done with you.

He was in a foul mood when he pushed open the back door of Bikini. The noise level up front was deafening, and he could hear rhythmic clapping to the Brazilian dance number that was on. Dev threaded his way through the back, nodding at Maurizio, Carlos the busboy and Eddie the dishwasher.

The latest bikini girl was putting on quite a show. She was up on the bar, dancing barefoot for a wildly appreciative crowd, and many of the men showed their appreciation of her talents by slipping bills into her exceptionally small bikini bottom.

Occasionally Lila glanced up at her in disdain, but the crowd loved her. And they seemed to be a very thirsty crowd.

Dev spotted Pete over in the left front corner, and waved at him. Pete shot him a thumbs-up, letting him know that everything was cool tonight, no problems.

Dev mouthed a *thank you* and gestured for Pete to join him. He headed to his office, a tiny room that fit a small desk, two chairs and a file cabinet. In the only leftover space were stacked liquor boxes full of stuff for the bar. It was a bad idea to give the staff open access to them.

It wasn't a great idea to give himself open access to them, either, but Dev unearthed the Johnnie Walker Black Label from the pile and pulled out a bottle.

"Uh-oh," Pete said, as Dev slammed it onto his desk and went in search of a couple of cups. "What's up, Gig?"

"Nothing."

"Did your hot date not go well?"

"It was friggin' perfect," Dev said, slapping the cups onto his desk and unscrewing the top of the Black Label. He slopped some into both cups and pushed one toward Pete.

"Yeah, I can tell," Pete said in mild tones. "Listen, bud. You don't want to drink that."

"Yes, I do."

"No, you really don't. Remember how you're not going to be that guy anymore? The boozehound who does stupid crap because he drinks hard liquor?"

"Mind your own business, Pete."

"Funny," his friend responded, "but you asked me to come here and mind *yours* tonight while you had a date."

"Look, I'm only having one drink."

"One triple. And that's how it always starts."

Dev sighed and looked into the amber liquid for a long time. Then he pushed the cup away. "Damn you, Pete."

"Hey, you want to end up in some rehab joint?"

Dev shook his head. And it could easily come to that, he knew. He could handle wine and beer. But liquor needed to fade into history for him. It was as simple as that.

Recently, only a few days after Mark's wedding, he'd started one morning with a pitcher of Bloody Marys, and ended up over at the medical school plastering the bulletin board outside the dean's office with revealing pictures from Mark's bachelor party. A great prank on his friend Adam. Except Adam hadn't considered it very funny, and when Dev had sobered up, he'd realized it was an incredibly jerky thing to do.

"So, if your date was so perfect, then why are you in such a piss-poor mood?" Pete asked.

Dev reluctantly told him the tall fish tale.

Once he'd finished laughing his ass off, Pete was sympathetic in the way only guys can be. "You're an idiot," he said.

"Yeah, thanks. I'd figured that out all by myself."

"You have to win back her trust."

"How?" Dev asked hopelessly.

"Beats the hell out of me," Pete said.

"You're a lot of help."

"You got an excuse to see her again? She leave her panties behind, or anything?"

"Not even a thread," Dev said gloomily. "But she's coming to the grand opening—"

"Well, there you go!"

"As my account manager."

"Your what?"

Dev filled him in.

"Aw, jeez, McKee. You didn't tell me that part. You're an even bigger moron than I thought, man."

Dev reached for the Black Label again, but Pete snatched it away. "None of that. You want to drink and dial? Drink and be a douche?"

Dev slumped in his chair.

"Tell you what. This grand opening is going to be a fantastic fiesta, and you're the star of the show. You work the room, smile a lot, be confident and charm her all over again. Me and the guys, we'll make sure to say great things about you—"

"Are there any?"

"—and show her a good time."

"Not *too* good a time," Dev said, with a threatening squint.

"Not like that, man. Would we do that to you?"

"Probably."

"Okay, we would. Payback for the past. But we won't. I'll talk to the rest of the guys. We've got your back on this one."

"I can't thank you enough, man. She's—" Dev stared at his shoes. "She's real important to me. Hell if I know why, but she is."

21

KYLIE SHOWED UP AT BIKINI at 3:00 p.m. Monday, without giving any advance warning. It was better to do it this way, so that Dev didn't have a chance to obscure or hide anything about his records or finances that he might otherwise have obscured or hidden.

The nature of the bar-restaurant business already made it easy to skim off or hide cash, because so much of the stuff flowed in. Kylie wasn't naive. Dev, with his ability to manipulate the truth, probably had a safe full of greenbacks that he didn't intend to report to anyone, least of all the federal government.

Other than that, he'd probably have immaculate records that noted an appropriately low level of cash coming in.

Kylie pushed the hair off her forehead, straightened her skirt and pulled open Bikini's front door. It took her eyes a moment to adjust to the dim lighting, and she gratefully inhaled the cooler, dryer air. Outside, the heat and humidity were like a sticky blanket.

"Ah, it is the health inspector," said a faintly mocking and heavily accented voice from behind the bar. She recognized one of Dev's employees from the kitchen, the guy who'd made a spanking motion with his spatula the last time she'd been here.

"Yes," she said, flushing and trying to remember what fake name she'd used. Katherine Something, she thought, but couldn't be sure. "Is Mr. McKee here, please?"

"Momento," the guy said, wiping his hands on a towel. He emerged from behind the bar. "This way." He gestured for her to follow him.

Kylie hitched her bag higher on her shoulder and did so. Dev was in his tiny office with one hand clamped on to the phone at his ear and the other clamped to his face in evident frustration. "No," he said, *"not cool.* The grand opening is *this Saturday.* Your guys were supposed to be here last week. Then they were supposed to show this morning. They're not here, and I still have trim carpenters coming in and then painters through Friday!"

He listened for a moment to whoever was on the other end of the line. "Diego. Listen to me, you sack of shit. I don't care whether you and your little old *granny* have to get over here and finish the floor yourselves—you gotta make this happen. And you gotta make it happen starting in about an hour. I don't *care* whether you're behind on other jobs. I don't care *what* crew you've gotta pull off *what* other job. Invitations are out, my whole business is riding on this, the bank is breathing down my neck. You get your asses over here *now."*

He listened again.

"Yeah, not my problem."

More listening.

"Okay, fine. Yes, I will make it worth their while if they work all night. But they've gotta show the hell up. *Yesterday."* Devon slammed the phone into its cradle. "Motherfu—"

Spatula Guy cleared his throat. "Lady from health department is here, boss."

Dev spun around in his chair, startled.

Spatula Guy winked, to Kylie's annoyance. "You know, to inspect the 'frigerator again, eh?"

"Thank you, Maurizio. You can get on with the prep work for the bar, now."

"Sure, boss." The man gave an insolent two-fingered salute and sauntered away, but not before giving her a thorough once-over with his eyes.

"To what do I owe this honor?" Dev asked.

"The bank. I'm here to breathe down your neck," Kylie said sweetly.

"I don't remember you calling to make an appointment."

She didn't turn a hair. "No, but I figured I'd better look at your records before the grand opening."

He nodded tersely. "Okay. You do that." He rose and walked to the single filing cabinet. He pulled open the top drawer. "Have at it."

She looked in to an overflowing, horrific mess of random receipts.

"The second drawer down is full, too," Dev told her.

Kylie's jaw worked, but she couldn't even begin to express her feelings.

"Is there a problem?" he asked, when she hadn't said anything for a minute or two.

"Have you ever heard of, say, Quicken?"

"Yeah, I've been meaning to get that. Been too busy."

"Or maybe Excel?"

He shrugged.

"Or even an old-fashioned *ledger?*"

"Sorry you don't approve, but this is my system so far."

"This is not a system." She ground the words out from between clenched teeth. "This is— This is *chaos.*"

"All the bar receipts are in these four tequila boxes over

here," he said as if he hadn't heard her. "That's every drink or potato skin that's been sold since we opened a year ago."

"Then what are these?" Kylie pointed at the file cabinet.

"Those are receipts for everything *bought* for the bar, from two-by-fours to Tanqueray."

"Did you not file a tax return?"

"Got an extension. No time to deal with that crap."

"I see." Slowly she sank into the visitor's chair, disbelief permeating every pore of her skin. She dropped her bag on the floor and dragged her hands down her face. "Dev, how did you plan on running a business while ignoring all your paperwork?"

"I was going to bring in a bookkeeper, but I can't justify the cost of one yet."

"How do you even *know* that?" Kylie stared from the file cabinet to the boxes and then back again.

"I keep a running total in my head of what we've spent versus what we've brought in."

"Right," Kylie said, nodding. "In your *head*."

"Why the sarcasm?"

"Because that's not possible, Dev! There are thousands of receipts here. Unless you're some kind of Rain Man, you can't have any idea of what's going on with your business."

"Bet me," he said, his chin in the air.

"And I'll tell you something else," she said as if he hadn't spoken. "There is no way in hell that I can authorize the second loan payment without having clear records of what's going on with the money. Forget it."

"Fine," said Dev. "But I challenge you—I will give you approximate figures of what we've brought in and what's been spent for each month, and I'll bet you that they're good—give or take a couple of hundred bucks."

"Give or take a couple of hundred bucks," she repeated. "That's not exactly chump change."

Dev shrugged. "I'm an entrepreneur, not a bean counter."

Dear God in Heaven. "Do you have Excel on that computer?" Kylie asked, pointing at his desk.

"Yeah. I think so."

Kylie took a deep breath, then another. "Fine. Is every single receipt you have in those drawers and boxes?"

"Yeah. I'm real good about that. I pull 'em out of my desk and pockets every day before leaving."

"How orderly of you."

He shot her a glance full of annoyance, as if he had any right.

Kylie stared right back at him, her mind spinning furiously. She hadn't taken herself off the account immediately, as she should have, given her conflict of interest. So it was even more crucial that *nothing*—not a decimal—be out of order here. Her job at Sol Trust was at stake; not to mention her reputation and the course of her career in banking.

"I'm taking over your office for as long as I need to straighten out this mess," she announced, knowing full well that this decision would have a full impact on her other accounts.

"What about your other responsibilities?"

"Not your concern." She'd take a few personal days if she had to; plead a nasty flu. This was too dire a situation to ignore.

She stood, removed her suit jacket and draped it over his chair. Then she grabbed an armload of receipts and sat, spreading them over his desk and beginning to sort them by category and date.

"Make yourself at home," Dev said, his hands on his hips.

Kylie pointed at the door. "You. If you want my help, then you will get me a coffee with cream and sweetener. Other than that, don't show your face in here."

DEV WAS HALF-TEMPTED to pick her up, chair and all, and toss her out the window. The woman had a nerve, kicking him out of his own friggin' office and ordering him to fetch her coffee.

On the other hand, she was saving his ass, and he knew it. He hated the minutiae of paperwork, and hadn't thought too hard about it before opening Bikini—he'd figured he'd hire someone. But bringing in thirsty customers had been his top priority, and so he'd spent money on scantily clad bikini babes rather than clerical help.

He'd figured that he'd get around to the paperwork soon enough. But weeks had turned into months, and months into an entire year, and by then the job was so awful and hairy and overwhelming that he'd continued to ignore it.

Still, she didn't need to waltz in here and treat him like a derelict or something. He knew he was making a profit. A pretty tidy one. And he was slowly paying down his debt. He owed money to credit cards and several friends. But he made his monthly loan payment to Sol Trust, no problem. And he did keep a running total, monthly, in his head. Whether she believed him or not. Was it down to the exact penny? No. But Dev didn't operate that anal-retentively, and he never would.

So Miss Stick-Up-the-Butt in there could insult him all he wanted to—

Shit. Yeah, sure. It didn't matter if she insulted him. But it did matter if she refused to authorize the second part of the loan. Because he wouldn't be able to pay for the build-out of the restaurant, or for the grand opening party. And all those bills were net either thirty or sixty days.

He could go bankrupt and lose his condo.

So he, Dev, had better suck it up and get her that coffee, and make sure it was still piping hot when he served it to her.

Damn it.

But to save face, he ran the estimates in his head again and scribbled the numbers on a scrap of paper, which he handed to her. "Here. Let me know if these numbers are off by more than a couple hundred. I guarantee you they're not."

22

THREE DAYS, THIRTEEN designer coffees and a few sandwiches later, Kylie had chronologically and categorically organized, entered and totaled every single receipt and check in Dev's office. The tequila boxes were empty, their contents neatly stashed in folders in the immaculate file drawers.

While they'd barked at and taunted each other each time he'd dared to stick his head inside the office, the hostilities had evolved into an almost affectionate banter, and when Dev walked in on Friday morning he found that he missed her.

She'd insulted his intelligence, his business sense and his complete lack of responsibility or organization, but she'd been kind enough to bail him out of administrative hell. Why, he still didn't know. All he knew was that he was exceptionally horny, and she'd smacked his hands every time he'd ventured to put them on her.

Which was truly unfair, since on Tuesday she'd been wearing snug jeans instead of a business suit, and her ass had looked mouthwatering in them. Wednesday it was shorts and he'd drooled over her legs. Yesterday she'd bludgeoned him with a skimpy sundress because the temperature had been in the nineties for the second day in a row.

He'd crept up behind her and looked down the top of it.

She'd either heard or sensed him there and smacked him in the face with a manila file folder.

"Stop looking down my dress."

"Can't help it," Dev complained. "It's small. And well-ventilated."

"You're so juvenile," she said, busily typing in numbers one-handed and flipping through receipts with the other.

"You're so deliciously—and annoyingly—grown-up." His fingers slithered of their own accord around the back of the chair and under her arm until he held a breast in his ecstatic palm. He heard her breath hitch. Then—

"Put that down," she ordered, still ripping through figures on the keyboard.

"But I'm horny," Dev whined, sounding even to his own ears like a thwarted child.

"If you do not remove your hand from my breast, I will lean on the delete key and trash this entire Excel file. Then you can start over with inputting the receipts, Mr. Hunt-and-Peck."

"But Kylie, you seem tense," Dev told her, complying unwillingly and only after he'd deliberately brushed a thumb over her nipple. It popped to attention instantly, he was happy to see. "I can help you with that...."

She snorted.

His hands slithered to her neck and shoulders, and he began to massage. She gave in for a couple of moments, rolling her head forward and letting him ease her muscles.

Yes! He bent forward to inhale the floral scent of her hair.

"Are you sniffing me? Like a dog?"

He snapped upright. "Of course not."

She turned and looked at him suspiciously. "I think you were."

He tried to look as innocent as possible, but was sure he'd

failed miserably. Especially when she put a hand in the center of his chest and shoved, stiff-arming him away from her.

"You need to back off, Dev. I'm trying to do you a favor, here."

"Yes, you are, though I'm not sure why. And I'm trying to thank you in the only way I know how." He aimed a smile at her that was calculated to disarm. It failed.

"Why?" she repeated, frowning. She sat silent for a moment as if trying to figure it out herself. Then she shrugged. "I'm trying to protect the bank's investment, that's all."

"This is all about money? About your job?"

"Of course. Why? What do you think it's about?"

"I have a suspicion that you don't do this for every client of the bank."

"You're right about that. Most clients don't let their businesses get into this hellacious state."

"You sure you're not giving me some special treatment, here?"

"Why would I do that?"

"Because you like me. Just a little."

"I do not like you," she said in tones of aggravation. "You're a disorganized wreck. And you're a liar."

"I'm a fish fabler. You're the liar. Because you do like me, Kylie. C'mon. Admit it." He donned his most charming smile and eased closer to her. He bent his head so that his face was angled directly above hers, and she stared into his eyes, uncertainty creeping into hers.

He kissed her. He couldn't help himself. Her lips were warm, soft and coffee-flavored. They yielded to his, opened to his. Then her hand shot out again and pushed against his chest. "No, Dev. We're keeping this just business."

He lifted his head reluctantly. "Why?"

She shook her head mutinously but didn't answer.

"Why?"

"Because there's a serious conflict of interest, here, Dev. I have to make a decision on whether to sign off on a second loan installment to you, and I cannot make that decision while sleeping with you. Why won't you get that through your skull?"

He just looked at her.

"I could get *fired*," she said. "I'd be fired if anyone at the bank knew that I'd slept with you while handling your account."

"And which way are you leaning?" Dev asked.

"On the loan installment?"

"Yes."

"I don't know," she said, and massaged her temples as if she had a headache. "On the one hand, I have to tell you that your organizational skills throw up a zillion red flags that you aren't a responsible businessperson. On the other..."

"Did you find any discrepancies? Anything that didn't add up? Did you find that my estimates were within a couple hundred dollars per month, like I told you?"

She nodded slowly. "I haven't found anything that doesn't add up. No expense outlays that don't make sense. No missing funds. No extra cash, either."

Dev felt a quiet sense of triumph. "And what does that tell you, Kylie?"

"That you're handling things pretty well, over all."

"And what else does it tell you?"

"That...you're honest."

"Ah. You sound surprised."

She shrugged uncomfortably.

Dev folded his arms across his chest and glowered at her. "You know what, Kylie? I won't be trying to look down your dress anymore. Because out of all the not-so-nice things you've assumed about me and said to me, that hurts the most. Did you come in here for the last three days to help me, really?

Or did you come in here so that you could prove to yourself that I was crooked and justify your fear of getting involved with me?"

Kylie looked stricken. She opened her mouth and then closed it.

"Yeah. You think about that." He walked to the door and opened it. "And maybe, when you're ready to be honest about your own fear of getting hurt again, then you'll get in touch with me. Until then, don't you even *think* about calling me a liar."

Dev hadn't slammed the door behind him. He'd shut it quietly, but with finality.

KYLIE HAD FINISHED INPUTTING the last numbers into Excel and then ran totals and estimates for future revenue. She studiously refused to think about what Dev had said to her. Instead she compartmentalized it and blocked any emotional reaction to it until she was done with the task at hand.

The numbers looked good. As long as Dev brought someone in for a few hours a week to keep up with his paperwork—and he could afford someone part-time—she had no reason to deny him the second installment of the loan from Sol Trust.

That brought her some measure of relief, since the numbers were in black and white—unlike her feelings.

Kylie cleaned off Dev's desk and packed up her things, then went looking for him to tell him the good news. But he was nowhere to be seen. The painters were finishing up the final touches on trim in the restaurant space, which was gorgeous.

The place was all Italian modern, full of elegant curves and warm wood, from the lighting to the free-standing walls to the furniture. It was painted in a palette of soft blues and greens with an occasional splash of bright turquoise. Surprise accents of bright yellow appeared sparingly here and there. Banquettes and chairs were upholstered in deep blue.

The total effect conjured images of ocean and sunshine, which fit in well with the South Beach location. But the marine theme was only hinted at. It was all subtle and elegant, sexy and imaginative.

The tables for Saturday were already set up, with white cloths, sparkling glassware and gleaming silver. By then most of the strong paint odor would have faded, though the whole place smelled new. No harm in that.

Dev had to be a bundle of nerves about the opening, but he hid it well. Kylie stood for a moment longer, then nodded at the painters and went through the door that connected restaurant to bar. She stuck her head into the kitchen, the office again and even braved the giant refrigerator, but there was no sign of Dev.

So she left. She blinked in the sudden light and heat outside and rounded the corner of the building. And there he was, one shoulder propped up against the wall, sucking hard on a cigarette.

She suddenly felt shy and didn't know what to say to him. She hadn't processed her feelings—they were still in the vault.

When he saw her, he pulled the cig from his mouth and blew out a gray, toxic cloud. "I really don't smoke much."

She lifted a shoulder. "I'm not your mother."

"No. You're the big, bad bank lady." He lifted a corner of his mouth.

"Not so big. Not so bad. Everything looks good, Dev. I'll sign off on the second installment."

He nodded, then took a drag on the cigarette and squinted at her before spouting smoke again. "Thanks. Really. I mean it. For everything you've done."

"You're welcome. No worries."

He let out a short, unamused bark of laughter. Then took another drag and spewed out smoke. "No worries? Yeah, right."

"You nervous about Saturday?"

"What do you think?"

"I think it's going to be a huge success. And a success you deserve, Dev."

His mouth flattened and he gazed off into the distance. "I don't know about that."

"What do you mean?"

He shrugged.

And suddenly she knew exactly where his head was. She understood where, in fact, it had been for the past decade. She knew where all the partying, the obnoxiousness, the womanizing and the drinking had come from: a desire to lose himself. To forget who he'd been. Black out his inner torment over his friend's death.

He'd wanted, above all, to fall into the cocoon of a coma and emerge fresh, reborn, able to fly away from his guilt.

"Dev." Kylie put a hand on his arm. "Look at me. You can't keep beating yourself up about the past."

"Ha," he said, his dark eyes full of pain. "Somebody has to."

"No. That's not true. You were kids. Stupid ones, maybe. But *kids*. And Will's death wasn't your fault, no matter what his parents said to you in their grief. In fact, they owe you an apology, Devon."

Tears gathered in his eyes. "They don't."

"They do. But I'm not going to stand here and argue about it. I think you should send them an invitation to the opening."

His mouth dropped open. "Are you *high?*"

"Of course not."

"Then you're crazy."

"Send it, Dev. See what happens."

He changed the subject abruptly, and she let him. She'd done her best, and now she had to go.

Kylie reached up and touched his cheek with her hand.

"The restaurant looks stunning, Dev. And if the aromas over the past few days are anything to judge by, the food will be incredible."

"Let's hope so. If the chef and the rest of the staff don't come to blows."

She smiled. "Bodvar *is* a little hyper." On her way to the ladies' room, she'd witnessed him pelting Maurizio with bits of onion, apparently because he didn't like the way it was sliced.

"A little? Jeez, the guy will be the death of me. Him and Lila, with her temper tantrums and that damned jealous boyfriend of hers."

She noticed that the hand holding his cigarette was shaking almost imperceptibly. The other was shoved deep into the pocket of his jeans. Sweat beaded at his temples and on his lip.

"It's going to be fine, Dev. Really." She put a hand on his arm.

"You're going to be here, right?" His dark eyes held an almost feverish intensity. "No matter what."

She'd known the *what* referred to their earlier conversation and the uncertainty of their relationship. She'd let that remain unresolved, because she simply hadn't known how to resolve it. "Of course I'll be here. I wouldn't miss it for the world."

23

As EIGHT O'CLOCK approached on Saturday night, Dev told himself that he wasn't nervous. Everything was going smoothly. His sister Ciara, who worked for a PR firm, had sent out follow-up press releases, gotten him radio spots and even a couple of regional TV spots that had advertised the event, so that they'd draw the curious to the bar side and pique their interest even if they weren't officially invited to the dinner.

Ciara had rushed in at six with boxes and boxes full of goody bags for the guests, stuffed with enticing products.

These currently sat in colorful rows on a table at the rear, and to either side stood a champagne fountain that would be operated by—who else?—two stunning models in bikinis and spike heels.

While the bar would serve as usual, waiters would circulate the restaurant side with trays of wine, champagne and hors d'ocuvres during the cocktail hour. At nine o'clock, the guests would be asked to take their seats for a multi-course dinner.

They'd start with a chilled avocado soup followed by tiny crab cakes. Then a salad of baby field greens misted with Bodvar's signature Bikini dressing.

The main course was a lobster-stuffed sole with a delicate white-wine sauce, served over a truffle-infused couscous.

Those allergic to shell fish were slated for filet mignon with chanterelle-shitaki risotto.

And dessert? A choice of lemon cheesecake or a light-as-air chocolate-raspberry swirled mousse.

The restaurant, at capacity, could serve one hundred and sixty diners, and they had RSVPs for almost every seat. The VIP attendees included—but weren't limited to—the hotel heiress twins and their dates, a huge pop star and her entourage, a bevy of models, a couple of major developers, a senator and his social secretary/mistress, a major magazine publisher, some big retailers, a yacht-builder, a few industry leaders and a former wrestler-turned-film-star known affectionately as the Boulder, whose date was his fourteen-year-old daughter. Last, but not least, they'd invited a couple of newspaper columnists in the hopes of a mention in the *Herald* or *Sun Sentinel*.

It was a given that some of these people wouldn't show up despite promising to attend, in which case Dev would lure in some beautiful people off the street, seat them carefully and pray that they behaved themselves.

He looked at his watch and went to check on things in the kitchen, where Bodvar and Maurizio were barely speaking and the other staff were keeping their heads ducked and their shoulders hunched behind growing piles of crab shells and legs. Bodvar insisted that all ingredients be fresh and refused to buy shelled crabmeat or lobster meat since he couldn't be sure how old it was.

Dev had refrained from pointing out that the crabs and lobsters themselves could have been frozen for any length of time before they were put out at the fish market. It didn't seem wise.

The poor bastards in the kitchen had been there since the early hours of the morning, slicing and scooping out avocados for the soup. They'd then progressed to deboning the fish and cracking open the lobster.

Yesterday they'd prepped all the vegetables and worked on sauces. They'd baked the cheesecakes the day before. Everyone looked exhausted. Truth to tell, they looked as if they'd like to stuff Bodvar bodily into the giant oven and serve his head as a centerpiece.

Dev couldn't blame them. Bodvar was a maestro with food, but he was a lousy people person. And he was even more jacked up today than usual, bouncing on his toes, twitching and screaming what sounded like Swedish obscenities. He'd been up all night, for sure. And his whole reputation, like Dev's, was riding on the success of this event.

Still, there was no violence other than verbal. No blood. So Dev went to check on Lila and the backup bartenders, one a stacked little blonde named Judy and one a long-haired guy from Texas named Bobby Ray. Everything seemed under control.

At eight Dev's buddies arrived, including Pete, Adam and Jay. Adam was still annoyed at Dev for the medical school prank, but at least he was speaking to him and was here to support him. He'd asked them to come early so that the first guests wouldn't feel as if, well, they were the first guests. Dev sent everyone over to the bar for free drinks.

At eight-thirty, his mom and dad showed with his brother and his wife to kick off the McKee Family Circus. Mami, at fifty-two years old, looked thirty-eight at most. Her black hair streamed to her caramel shoulders, her huge dark eyes needed little makeup and if he hadn't seen her bruising the day after her discreet lid lift, he'd never have believed she'd had one.

Mami had a figure to die for and an emotional range that rivaled a roller coaster, which was probably why Dev dealt so patiently and effectively with Lila the moody bartender. Mami was also an incorrigible *chismosa,* or busybody. She could charm the skin off a snake, but there was a reason he kept his file cabinets and desk locked and didn't talk about business around her.

Dev hurried over and whistled appreciatively at her form-fitting, plunging red cocktail dress and spiked heels while she preened. Then he kissed her cheek and clapped his long-suffering Irish father on the back. "Dad, you're looking good."

This was an egregious lie. His father snorted and patted the large belly that copious amounts of home-cooked Cuban food and gallons of Irish whiskey had cultivated. "Right. Your mother just told her sister that I'll give birth to twins next month."

Mami whipped her head around. "Ay! I say no such theeng."

"You think I don't oonderstand Spanish after therty yares with ya, woman?" Dad shot back in his Irish brogue.

"Mami, have a glass of champagne. Dad?"

"Bubbly piss," his father said with disgust. "No. Jameson's, rocks. Before I go into labor, eh?" He shot his wife a dirty look and Dev edged him away with a pleading glance toward Pete.

"Señor McKee," Pete boomed out. "Lila was just asking how you are. She's got a whiskey with your name on it."

One disaster averted, Dev offered champagne to his sister-in-law and asked after his small nephews. His brother Aidan, a professor of comparative religion, looked around in appreciation. "Place looks great, Devster. Who knew you had taste?"

"Hey, I saved all the leftover eighties fabric for you, bro. I figured you might take up quilting."

"How'd you guess?"

"You want a real drink, or you want bubbly piss?" Dev made a wry face and gestured toward the champagne fountain.

"Got a good cabernet?"

"Of course." Dev hijacked a waiter's tray and supplied his

brother with the wine, as a commotion of noise and flashbulbs started at the main entrance. "Excuse me."

An ex-Miami Dolphins player and his wife had arrived, and it looked as if a photographer and reporter from one of the newspapers had, too.

Dev greeted everyone and made sure they got drinks right away. More people followed: friends, business acquaintances, VIPs. As the room filled and people seemed to be having a good time, he relaxed a little.

He stuck his head into the bar and was pleased to see that everything was going smoothly there. At least five men leaned on the bar, riveted by Lila's assets. These were showcased in a skin-tight, electric-blue sequined camisole—worn Miami-style. In other words with no bra, nipples plainly visible under the clingy, sparkly material.

Dev winked at her and was rewarded with a soulless black stare and a toss of her mane. He departed for the kitchen and was less reassured by what was going on in Bodvar's domain.

First, it was hotter than July in the Sahara. The ovens produced waves of shimmering, suffocating heat. Curls of white steam wafted up from ten different pots, creating an aromatic but stifling stainless-steel bowel of hell.

Towering over his sweating, cowering minions was a Satanic blond Bodvar, perspiration and menace rolling down his irate face and soaking his collar and the brim of his tall hat. His eyes rolled maniacally in his head, the whites showing.

Dev squinted at him. If he didn't know better—

No. Don't even think it.

But the guy showed every sign of using amphetamines.

At his feet was an overturned pan in a lake of tomato sauce flecked with onions and spices, which looked like nothing so much as a pool of blood and gore. Had he thrown it down in a fit of temper?

On the counter next to him were two sheets of blackened, burned bruschetta.

"What's going on, here?" Dev asked.

Bodvar yelled something having to do with incompetence, laziness, stupidity. Since this was in half-English, half-Swedish and peppered with foul words in both, Dev didn't understand it all, but it was pretty easy to get the gist of it.

"Okay, everyone. Let's calm down and get the mess cleaned up. Get the bruschetta remade and back into the ovens."

Bodvar roared that there was no more bread. Dev held up a finger and pulled out his cell phone, hitting speed dial for Ciara. Could she stop at a grocery's bakery on her way and bring about ten baguettes? Sure. Problem solved.

Bodvar lashed out about the poor quality of grocery store-baked bread. Plus baguettes were French, not Italian. "That," Dev told him, "can't be helped. Make sure the topping is good and we'll hope not everyone is as picky as you."

Without a word of thanks, his chef invited him, not so politely, to leave his kitchen immediately. Since thirty minutes before the grand opening was not the time to fire him, Dev complied only to find three waiters in the back making extremely free with sixteen-ounce plastic cups of champagne from the fountains.

Unfortunately, now was not the time to fire them, either. He did take away their cups and kick their butts back into service, but he was afraid the damage had been done. There were eight waiters in all, and his professional eye detected that seven of them were at least somewhat impaired, judging by their rolling gaits and goofy grins. Great. Just friggin' great.

Dev snagged them, one by one, and whispered violently that he didn't want to hear any confessions, but if he saw them within a foot of any alcohol again that night, he'd personally dismember them and toss them in the Dumpster behind the restaurant.

He begged the one sober guy, who was in his forties, to help police the rest of them.

Dev headed back to his guests and worked the room, which had filled almost to capacity when Kylie made her entrance.

She was stunning in a sea-foam-green strapless chiffon dress with a long matching chiffon scarf wound around her graceful neck. She'd twisted her hair up into a loose knot and secured it with a silver clip. And she wore the same silver sandals that she'd worn to Mark's wedding—the ones of which he had very fond memories.

"Jesus, Mary and Joseph," Dev's dad exclaimed, swirling the whiskey in his glass. "And who's the goddess?"

Dev watched her walk in, watched the way the crowd parted for her and took note, whispering as she passed. Who was she? Not emaciated enough to be a model. Not trampy enough to be a pop star. Was she an up-and-coming designer? An actress from another country? A mogul's wife without her mogul?

Nope. She was his big, bad, bank lady.

Dev could feel himself grinning like an idiot. He couldn't help it. Because she was walking right toward him.

His dad gaped, fixated on the perfection of her face, the curve of her shapely calves, the swing of her graceful hips.

He almost tripped over his own feet himself as she approached, and had to lock his knees.

"Hello, Dev," she said with that Swiss-vault smile. "Congratulations on your grand opening." And she kissed him—on the cheek, to his disappointment.

24

DEV SMELLED WONDERFUL—of some sort of exotic woodsy aftershave. He'd dressed in Miami black, in an understated raw silk shirt and trousers with a European cut. His calfskin shoes had to be Italian, and were polished to a high shine. He looked like what he was: a successful restaurateur with a perhaps shadowy past.

"Be still my heart," rumbled the older gentleman standing next to Dev, and she turned toward him with a smile.

"Kylie, meet my father, Declan McKee. He's Irish, he'll soon be drunk, and you shouldn't trust him in any dark hallways. Dad, this is Kylie Kent, my...account manager at the bank. Keep your hands to yourself."

Declan managed to look wounded at the implication that he might be a rogue, but at the same time he rakishly waggled his eyebrows at her. She understood instantly how his son had acquired what she'd once called his peculiar, repulsive appeal.

"So good to meet you," she said, offering her hand.

"Dazzled," Declan said. "Charmed. Befuddled. Annihilated, actually."

"Oh, my." Kylie raised her eyebrows at Dev. "He's even more full of blarney than you are."

As Dev and his father laughed, a tiny but voluptuous

woman in low-cut red silk bustled over, leading with her bosom. She reminded Kylie of a slightly older version of Salma Hayek.

"Ay, Devonito, who is the beautiful lady?"

"Devonito?" Kylie teased him in a whisper, then turned.

"Mami, this is my account manager at the bank, Kylie Kent. Kylie, my mother, Maria Elena. She loves to exasperate her husband—"

"Hear! Hear!" said Declan, loudly.

"—and torment her children. Don't tell her anything that you don't want the entire city to know by morning."

Maria Elena rolled her eyes at the men. "Please," she told Kylie, "ignore his lies. Someone must—how you say?—keep the men in line. They are fools."

Kylie chuckled. "I'll drink to that." She raised the glass Dev had supplied and took a sip of champagne.

"Now. I have eyes. I see things. You manage more than my son's account, no?"

Kylie choked on the tiny bubbles she'd inhaled and began to cough. Dev smacked her lightly on the back.

"Yes, and very well," he said to his mother. "Come along now, Kylie. That's not a conversation you want to get into with Mami. Am I right?"

Grateful, she went with him, calling over her shoulder, "Very nice to meet you, Mrs. McKee."

"Ha," said the little scarlet diva. "You see? She is slipping with our son, Declan. Her face is red as the inside of a *sandía*. A watermelon."

"Oh, my God," Kylie moaned.

"My parents are a lot to handle," Dev said apologetically. "They're completely dysfunctional but that's the only way they know how to function. And neither of them could tolerate anyone else, so they're truly meant to be together."

"I see."

"Doubtful, but that's a taste of them, anyway." He laughed. He looked tense and worried; deep lines etched his forehead and dark circles had gathered under his eyes.

"You okay, Dev?"

"Yeah. Great. Especially now that you're here." He brushed her cheek with his knuckles, which sent a tingle through her. She told herself not to be touched by either the gesture or his words, but who was she kidding?

"Something's bothering you," she told him. "I can see it."

He blew out a breath. "We've got some tipsy waiters and a cranked-out, abusive chef who ejected me from the kitchen for peacekeeping. It's a little troublesome."

"A *little?*"

He shot her a tight grin as a guy she remembered as one of Mark's groomsmen walked over. "Hey, Pete. Kylie, you remember Pete from the wedding, right?"

"Of course." She smiled and extended her hand.

Pete caught it, folded it in and kissed her on the cheek. "And how could I forget *you?*"

It was the warm, sweet gesture of a teddy bear, not a slick move by an operator. She liked him immediately.

"Pete, here, is the guy I rely on when I need someone to look in on the bar. He's a lifesaver and a good friend." Dev clapped him on the shoulder and he shrugged good-naturedly. "Don't know what I'd do without—"

He was interrupted by an ominous clatter and curses from the kitchen.

"Uh-oh. I'd better check on that." Dev careened toward the noise as one of the waiters scrambled out, followed by two more. "Pete? Can you and the guys start getting everyone seated? It's after nine."

"Sure."

Kylie and Pete exchanged worried glances.

"I'll help," she said. "People just need to find their place cards, right?"

"Yeah."

A bad feeling drove her toward the kitchen first, though.

"Herre Gud! Du bondlurk!" she heard. "Get out! Get out of here, *Idioten!*"

"No, no, no. Guys, you're not leaving." This was Dev, his tone urgent. "You can't leave!"

"Hons Hjarna! Out, out, out! I'll kill you!"

"Shut up, Bodvar. Guys, you can't take off in the middle of our grand opening. You can't."

China shattered. Footsteps scrambled. She heard a door opening.

"You're killing me, guys. Come back here. I'll pay you double—"

Kylie pushed through the double doors of the kitchen to find a bunch of shattered white bowls on the floor in the middle of a creamy, pale green swamp.

"Please, Sergio, don't go. I will pay you triple if you stay through the night. And you, too, Bucky." Dev pleaded with the last two waiters, a forty-something guy and a sick-looking kid in his early twenties.

"Just ignore Bodvar," he said in an undertone. "He's on something. He's freaking out. I am begging you, don't leave me with nobody to serve this dinner."

The guy named Sergio nodded. "Okay, boss."

Bucky slowly nodded, too.

"Thank you," Dev said. "*Thank you.* Kid, go stick your finger down your throat in there and you'll feel better. Okay? Then wash up and get out here as soon as you can. People are starting to sit down. We've got to get the avocado soup out there while ballistic Bodvar finishes up the crab cakes."

"What can I do?" Kylie asked, as Dev turned, already rolling up his sleeves.

"You ever waited tables?" he asked, looking desperate.

"Yes. College."

"No. Forget it. I can't ask you to—"

But she was already sorting through the tuxedo parts and shirts on a nearby hanging rack. "Go get people seated. Send Pete and anyone else you can press into service back here. Will your mom and dad help?"

"Kylie, really—"

"Dev, find me five people at the very least. You have too much riding on this opening for us to let it fall apart. We can do this. Now, go get 'em."

"You're a goddess," he said, and ran out.

Kylie dealt first with Bodvar, who had stalked into the refrigerator and was sulking while he cooled off.

"Listen up, you," she said.

"Do not talk to me, health inspector lady!" he yelled.

"I *will* talk to you, and *you* will *shut the hell up,*" she said in quiet but deadly tones.

That got his attention. His blue eyes bulged and his lipless mouth dropped open.

"I'm not from the health department. I'm from the bank that has financed this restaurant. And if you do anything else to screw up this opening with your stupid histrionics, I will have a team of attorneys down on your ass so fast you won't even know what hit you. We'll sue you for hundreds of thousands of dollars in damages and get your Nordic ass deported. So you get out of this fridge and back to your pots and pans. Got it?"

He closed his mouth and glared at her from his superior height, not moving.

"Do you understand me?" Kylie shouted.

At last he muttered something incomprehensible under his breath and stomped past her.

For a horrible moment, she thought he'd walk out the door.

But her instincts paid off: the big bully didn't know what to do when he was the one being bullied.

"And don't you dare throw anything else on the floor," she added. "Or I'll push your face down into it and make you eat it, shattered crockery and all."

He made a rude gesture at her, but she ignored him and turned as all the groomsmen from Mark's wedding, plus Dev's parents, burst through the kitchen door, followed by a guy and two girls introduced as Dev's brother and sisters.

"Okay, everyone," Kylie said. "We're going to get dirty and sweaty, but we're going to run this thing smoothly. Each of you grab a tray of soups. You need to hold the tray with one hand and arm underneath it, and the other hand at the edge to steady it. I warn you—the trays will be very heavy. Mr. and Mrs. McKee, may I suggest that you stay in here and keep an eye on his holy Swedishness over there?"

They looked at each other and nodded.

Bodvar had become a whirling dervish, heating sauces and flipping huge pans of the stuffed sole in and out of ovens and warmers.

Dev grabbed a tray of soups and everyone else followed his lead. "Okay, guys. I'm going to deliver these and then steal a bartender from the other side, because one of the busboys took off with all the waiters."

"Dev," Kylie said, "I know you want to help, but you need to be out there circulating among the guests.

"*Si*, Devonito. Out with you. Go and charm everyone," his mother said. "We do this."

Dev looked at each and every one of them, his gaze lingering on Kylie's face. "You guys, thank you. I cannot thank you enough—"

"Shhhh, Dev. Get out there to the party." Kylie took the tray from him and gave him a push.

Then they all got to work. Kylie put the young waiter on

dishwashing duty, which meant the remaining volunteers had to serve twenty tables of eight. They delivered all the avocado soup, returned to the kitchen and helped to assemble the crab-cake appetizers.

"Remove the soup bowl from the left, serve the crab cakes from the right," Kylie reminded them. "And whatever you do, don't drip anything on the guests."

The amateur waiters were amazingly efficient, and some-how all of them worked together in the steamy, high-stress, aromatic kitchen to get the main courses plated and delivered to the diners, who, with only a couple of exceptions, were very happy with the food.

One of the hotel heiresses sent back her fish, and the Boul-der's teenage daughter wanted her filet a little less pink in the middle. Kylie held her breath while Bodvar turned purple in the face, but to his credit he didn't even curse or spit on the girl's entrée. He muttered and threw it on the grill, asking sar-castically if she wanted him to pour ketchup on top before he sent it out again.

And Dev's parents might have an odd, dysfunctional rela-tionship, but to her shock his family was stable—like him—and was pulling together to help him. Who could have known?

Kylie peeked out of the porthole doors and saw Dev squeeze the pop star and pose for a photographer. Then he kissed her cheek and moved on to chat with the mayor. Satis-fied that everything was going well, she gulped from a bottle of icy cold water, blotted her forehead and temples with a paper towel and looked ruefully down at her formerly gor-geous sea-foam-green dress, which was dotted and splotched with crab, remoulade and port wine sauce.

She blotted up what she could, and then made a quick run to the ladies' room. It was on her way back to the kitchen that she saw him.

"Kylie?" The door to the men's room literally hit her ex-fiancé in the butt as he gaped at her.

She pushed her wilted hair out of her face and desperately wished that she'd touched up her lipstick and powdered her nose before leaving the bathroom.

She glanced down at her dress again, in dismay. "Jack," she said faintly. "What are you doing here?"

25

As DESSERT AND COFFEE were served by his team of amazing friends and relatives, Dev made a speech that people later told him was urbane and witty and welcoming.

All he knew was that he thanked everyone for coming to help him launch Bikini: The Restaurant. But while the words poured out of his mouth in some semblance of a logical sequence, he couldn't take his eyes off Kylie. She'd pulled her hair back and she still wore her own silver sandals while she hustled tables and made sure everyone had everything they wanted.

He could tell by the way she moved—gingerly—that her feet must be killing her, and no wonder: the spiked heels on those shoes had to be four inches high. But she was still graceful, still smiling, still performing with complete efficiency and as if she wanted to do nothing more in the world than schlep desserts and cappuccinos.

In the middle of his big speech he realized that he was a hundred percent in love with her. Hopelessly, irretrievably, and utterly a goner.

It had nothing to do with her looks or her physical attributes. It had nothing to do with great sex. It had everything to do with her heart and her take-no-prisoners attitude; the fact that she never let anything beat her.

She'd walked into Mark's rehearsal dinner upset and hurting, only to hold her head high and proposition Dev. And even when he'd found her sniffling in a closet, she hadn't latched on to him as the next man to come along. No, she'd walked away without a backward glance. And then she'd given him hell when she thought he'd humiliated her.

When she'd discovered that she had to deal with him professionally, had she made excuses? No, she'd bearded the lion in his den.

Then she'd pulled the thorn out of the lion's paw by straightening out his business affairs, and only okayed the second installment of his loan when she was positive that he was handling the money honestly and responsibly.

Finally, she'd jumped in and saved the day this evening when all the waiters had left.

Dev stood in front of all one hundred and sixty guests and said, "So. I'd like to thank every single one of you for coming tonight, and I hope you'll revisit us often with your families, friends and business acquaintances." He paused and waited for the audience's clapping to subside.

"Finally, I'd like to express my immeasurable gratitude to everyone who's made this event possible. To the chef, to my regular staff, to my parents and friends, and to a very special lady here tonight from Sol Trust. Thank you from the bottom of my heart."

Kylie blushed red from her neck to the roots of her hair and disappeared into the kitchen. But not before making eye contact with him.

Dev stopped to chat with a few more people before making his way purposefully toward the back in search of her. He wanted to lay a big smacker right on her lips, lift her into the air and twirl around with her.

Only after setting her down would he deck his temperamental, if extremely talented, chef. That could wait.

Ciara approached him, her dark cap of hair shining, her hands full of extra goody bags. "Phew," she said, "thanks to Kylie, everything went very well. And—" she hesitated "—there's someone here to see you. Two people, actually. They're up front."

She put down the bags and led him by the hand through the crowd. Dev's heart pounded once, twice, and then lodged firmly in his throat. An older couple was silhouetted by the door, looking out of place and uncomfortable.

They turned and met his eyes: Will's parents. They were older and more care-worn, but it was them.

He stopped in his tracks; he didn't know who'd invited them. He hadn't had the nerve, in the end.

Will's dad swallowed hard and then stuck out his hand.

Dev took it, bemused.

"Congratulations."

"Th-thank you, sir."

Will's mother surged forward and folded Dev into her arms. "He'd be very proud of you, honey. Will would be here tonight."

Dev couldn't control the tremors that racked his body. He couldn't say a word. He just hugged her, hard, and tried to hold the tears back.

"See to your other guests, Devon," Will's mom said, finally pulling away. She put her hand on his shoulder. "We'll be in touch."

All he could do was nod as he watched them walk away.

"Ciara? What…? How…?"

"Kylie called me and asked me to send them an invitation. So I did."

Dev nodded again. Then the words escaped his lips before he could retract them. "I'm going to marry her."

"You're *what?*"

"I'm going to marry Kylie. You wait and see."

"If she'll have you," his sister said acidly.

"Trust me. I will spend my last breath talking her into it."

Dev didn't see Kylie in the crowd. He pushed through the throngs of people to the kitchen to find her, but Kylie wasn't there, either. He made for the double doors that led to where the restrooms were, and had pushed one six inches open when he heard Kylie say, "Jack. What are you doing here?"

KYLIE STARED AT HER EX, feeling discombobulated.

"I'm in the bar with a friend," Jack said. He looked ten years younger than he had when she'd seen him last. In those eight months, he'd lost a good twenty pounds, and there was color in his chiseled, handsome face. He wore a clean, pressed polo shirt and khaki pants instead of a grungy T-shirt and shorts with holes in them.

By contrast, she was conscious of the fact that she smelled like a Clydesdale, her makeup had steamed off and she resembled a drowned rat. No woman wanted to run into her ex looking this way. But she stood her ground and maintained her dignity.

"The men's room in the bar is occupied. So I crossed over to use this one." He was eyeing her strangely, and no wonder. "You look…good," he said lamely. "I've actually been meaning to call you."

There was a shock. "Jack, you don't have to lie. I look like absolute hell, but you would too if you'd been stuck in a restaurant kitchen and waiting tables."

"Why—"

"I'm helping out a friend. The entire waitstaff quit right before the opening tonight, so a bunch of us are pitching in." She shrugged.

"You were always a trooper, Kylie," Jack said. He shoved

his hands in his pockets and looked down at his shoes. "I— Listen. I really screwed up with you. I got off-track. Mixed up."

"Yeah," she said softly. "Well, it looks like you're doing really well, now."

"I'm off the pills," he said. "And, you know. The other."

"That's great. That's really great."

"I've been meaning to call. But I was embarrassed."

She wiped away some more sweat from her jaw, uncomfortable with the conversation. Uncomfortable around him. Weirded out, in fact. "Jack, you don't have to be embarrassed. Nobody's perfect. We all go through…things."

He nodded. "Thanks. I guess I want you to know that I'm sorry."

"It's okay, Jack." And she was surprised to realize that it was. How strange was that? She found herself looking at his all-American, close-to-perfect features: the square jaw, the wide-spaced light-blue eyes, the prominent cheekbones.

She'd kissed those lips, but couldn't remember exactly how it felt to do that. She'd held his hand, but couldn't feel much of a connection to him now. She felt wistful. Sorry for how things might have been. But was there anything else?

She wasn't sure.

"Well, I've got to get moving," she said cheerfully. "It was good seeing you."

"Will you let me take you to dinner next week, Kylie? I'd like to talk."

"Oh. Um…"

"Just for old times' sake?"

She felt conflicted. She didn't know if this was a good idea, but she had to get back to the kitchen, and didn't want to be hurtful. So she took the easy way out. "Okay. Call me and we'll figure out the details."

"Great," Jack said. "That's great." Then, before she could

dodge him, he leaned forward and gave her a quick kiss on the mouth. "Talk to you soon, babe."

Babe?

"Uh-huh," she said, then turned tail and ran back into the Ladies' room.

DEV FROZE BEHIND THE kitchen door, something greasy and black sliding around in his stomach.

The Jack-ass had kissed her. On the lips. And she was going out with him next week. Worse, Dev knew in his bones that it wasn't for *old times' sake.* The guy sounded like a born predator. Dev wished he could have seen his eyes, but Jack's back had been to him.

Kylie's tone of voice had been soft, forgiving. Tender, even. She'd almost married this man. And even Dev, biased against the jerk, had to admit that the side of him he could see was tan and muscular and good-looking—if you liked the whole Aryan thing he had going. The douche bag probably highlighted his hair.

Why would Kylie go out with him?

Clearly she was still in love with the bottom-feeder.

Between this catastrophe and seeing Will's parents, his emotions were chaos. Dev followed blind instinct and habit.

He headed straight for his office and the bottle of Black Label that waited for him inside. He locked the door behind him and found a big plastic cup.

BY THE TIME HE STUMBLED out, Dev was seeing double. Everything was blurry and swam in and out of focus as he made his way to use the facilities.

Whoa…he was able to get his zipper down all right, but the gap in his pants kept moving and he had a helluva time getting his dick out. But then he figured out that there were two of them, so no wonder it had been tough.

Dev looked down at them, very proud. He decided it could only be a good thing for a guy to have two dicks. It was double the urine storage and double the fun to be had with a girl. You also had a backup if anything went wrong with the first one, right?

Now, the only problem with having two of the suckers was that it seemed to be extraordinarily hard to aim. Especially with a trick urinal that kept dancing around. It veered to the right, then it moved to the left. It even bounced up and down.

Dev focused really, *really* hard on it, though, and was happy to say that he beat it. Not a single drop of liquid landed on any of his four shoes. He was a champ! He could take on any video game after this and kick some real ass.

He managed to stow both of his penises into his pants, wash all eighteen—or was it twenty?—of his fingers and peer into the mirror. "Uncle Sam," he said, pointing at his reflections, "wants you! Nope, you. No, wait. The first one of you."

For some reason, that was hilarious: Uncle Sam wanting any of him at all. Dev had to tell the guys about this. Oh, yeah, and he had a Swedish chef to kill.

Then he was going to hunt down all the missing waiters and harness them to a sleigh. He'd make them fly him around to various rooftops as he lashed them with a whip and yelled, "Yah! Yah!"

He stumbled out of the men's room and barged into the kitchen like Clint Eastwood into a Wild West saloon. There was loud music playing. A bunch of people were washing dishes and drinking wine and putting away food in large containers.

"Hi, ebryone!" Dev said.

"Hey, Dev. Where you been?" His brother approached, a dish towel slung over his shoulder.

"Tha's top secret," Dev announced, and then burst out laughing.

Aidan took his arm. "Have you been drinking, bro?"

"Only water. I schwear." Dev laughed again. "C-can't tell anyone."

"*Right.* Devvy, old man, I think I should drive you home."

"Nope. Gotta serve dessert first. Where'd it go? Hey, where's the sheesecake? And the moushe—the moothe, uh, the pudding shit?"

"We served dessert an hour and a half ago. Then everyone left. You're wasted, man."

But Dev had found and focused on the object of his affections. Kylie stood at the long, stainless-steel sink with Pete, their hands plunged up to the elbows in soapy water, washing pots and pans. Adam and Ciara were drying.

Pete said something that made Kylie laugh, and she scooped a handful of bubbles and dropped them on his head. Pete returned the favor with a handful of bubbles to her nose, and Kylie squealed, then sneezed.

Dev swayed on his feet. Kylie had made a date with the Jack-ash. And now she was with Pete, his friend Pete. They looked like they were having *way* too good a time washing dishes. He was scrubbing her pot. She was scrubbing his pan.

Pete could *not* have her. Pete was a very, very nice guy, but Dev was better and she was his. Kylie couldn't date Pete. No way.

Dev shuffled toward them on his four feet.

Aidan sprinted after him and took his arm, but Dev shook him off.

Ciara saw him coming and her face adopted that expression she used when she was worried. But she didn't have any reason to worry. This would all be fine. He just had to convince Kylie that he was a better man than Pete.

But Pete was a really, really nice guy. Everyone said so. How was he better than Pete? How could he convince Kylie that she should go out with him, Dev, and not his buddy with all the soap bubbles?

And then the answer came to him. Of course! Why hadn't he thought of it before?

"Kylie," he said loudly.

She turned; so did Pete. "Hey, Dev. Where have you been hiding yourself?"

"He's zall wrong for you," Dev declared.

"Who is?" she asked. But she looked guilty.

"Pete. And whass-hiss-face. But *I* am a prince among men. An' you know what else?"

She sighed. "What, Dev?" A peculiar expression on her face, now. But he needed to impart this vital information to her. Then she'd smile and come running. How could she not?

He nodded, secure in this knowledge.

He took a big step forward and spread his hands wide, magnanimously including the rest of his kitchen kingdom. Why shouldn't they know, too? Everyone would be impressed.

Dev took a deep breath and focused glassily on the woman whom he loved above all others. The woman whom he wished to bear his children. The woman who would soon be his future bride.

"I have two dicks," he announced proudly.

26

"Nooo," MOANED DEV. "I did not say that."

"Yes, you did." Ciara held out a glass of water and four ibuprofen tablets. "You said it loud and clear in front of about twelve people, including Mami and Dad."

"They must be so proud." Dev swallowed the pills and wished that God would unscrew his head and mash it in a trash compactor to put him out of his misery.

"Mami was horrified—just whirled around and ran out. Dad laughed until he couldn't move. We were all mortified for you."

"And what did Pete say?"

Ciara's face softened. "That Pete. What a sweetie. Without a blink, he said, 'I know, Devster. And they're both much bigger than mine.'"

Dev couldn't help a grin at that one. "He said that?"

"Yes, he did."

"What a good guy."

"You have nicer friends than you deserve."

"Probably." Dev closed his eyes and pulled the covers over his face. "And Kylie? What did she do?" He wasn't sure he wanted to know the answer.

"She patted your cheek and said she'd always known you

were a real man. Then you offered to *show* both your dicks to her, and she got out of Dodge pretty quick."

Dev curled into a fetal position under the covers. "Kill me?" he begged Ciara.

"Sorry, bro. You asked."

"Oh, God. I'll never drink again."

"About that, Dev…"

"You don't have to tell me. I'm done. If I ever slip up again, I'm checking into a rehab place. I kid you not. It's pretty clear to me that my liver can't process that shit anymore. I hurt it too bad in my misspent youth."

"Yes, you did." Ciara was silent for a while. Then she said, "Look. I'm sorry about Kylie's date."

"What date?" Dev flipped the covers off his face and squinted at her.

"You know. The date she made with that Jack guy. That's what set you off. That's when you started drinking."

Jack. How could he have forgotten? The horrible ex-fiancé. The prince of porn. She was going out with him.

"Didn't I just ask you to kill me?" Dev pulled up the covers again. "Could you get on with that, please?"

"Dev, it's not like all is lost because of one date."

"Jack is her friggin' ex-fiancé, Ciara. If she's seeing him again, I'm out of the picture. Not that I didn't seal my fate last night anyway."

"Dev, once you're feeling better, why don't you pick up the phone and call Kylie? You can apologize."

The thought made him cringe. "I'm not calling her, Ciara. Not after I made such a colossal ass out of myself. Shit—what the hell would I say to her?"

"Tell her the truth, Dev. That you found out she was going to see what's-his-face again and you got really upset. Then you got drunk."

"I'm not calling her," he said through the covers.

"Chicken."

"There's only so much humiliation a guy can inflict on himself. I'm done."

And Dev mashed his face into a pillow, begged the devil to switch heads with him and rocked himself back to sleep on big waves of shame.

KYLIE WONDERED HOW MUCH Dev's head hurt the next morning. She was half-tempted to pick up the phone and ask him, but the other half of her was so disgusted by his drunken performance that she didn't care.

She'd never seen him that way, and frankly, she never wanted to see him that way again. He'd looked so handsome and together at the beginning of the night. He'd been so grateful that she'd stepped in and helped him pull off a successful opening night—that speech of his had touched her to the core. He'd also managed to shake her up inside with that direct, determined gaze of his. As if he'd said, from across the room, that he was coming for her. That she was his.

Truth to tell, it had been a thrilling moment from an embarrassing, primal, feminine point of view. The caveman preparing to drag his chosen woman off to his lair; promising to club a tasty varmint for her every day for the rest of her life.

From a slightly more romantic point of view, she'd felt like Cinderella must have when the prince strode toward her with the missing glass slipper.

But in the fairy tale, Prince Charming didn't disappear with it and consume a gallon of liquor. The prince didn't then reappear and announce to Cinderella that he had two dicks.

She'd never seen anyone make a bigger ass out of himself. And why? They'd pulled off a smashing success of a grand opening. He had been in the clear. The guests had been happy and prepared to spread the word to all their friends. Bikini was off and running.

So why had Dev felt the need to slink into his office like some weasel and glug down half a bottle of whatever? Celebrate by himself in the dark?

Who knew? But it wasn't impressive.

Kylie, girl. You really can pick 'em, can't you? A pill-popping porn addict and a smart-ass, accounting-averse drunk... with two dicks.

She wondered if Dev would call to apologize, and decided that if he did, she wouldn't answer. She didn't know what to say to him.

And then there was Jack. She didn't really want to have dinner with him, but she'd do it for one lowly reason: vanity. He'd seen her at her absolute worst. And from a purely female point of view, that was unacceptable. There were certain inalienable rights a woman had when it came to her ex...and the first one was that she looked like a million bucks should she ever run into him.

But Kylie went to work on Monday dreading Jack's phone call. She didn't like the way he'd called her *babe* on Saturday night. She didn't like the proprietary kiss he'd planted on her before walking away. And she especially didn't like what got delivered to the office at around 11:00 a.m.

April, the receptionist, called her cubicle to say there was a surprise waiting for her downstairs.

A surprise? That sounded ominous. Was it another embarrassing practical joke from Dev? Probably. She took a sip of lukewarm coffee—the air-conditioning vent above her desk had worked its usual wonders on her hot beverage—and walked to the elevator.

When it opened to let her out on the ground floor, she was greeted by who else? Milty Goldman and the same group of investment bankers in interchangeable suits who had witnessed the inflatable doughnut debacle.

"Miss Kent," boomed Milty.

"Hello, Mr. Goldman. Gentlemen. How are you this morning?"

"Fine, fine," Milty said genially, all the while doing a full-body scan of her, and not being too subtle about it. The rest of them did the same thing, and she felt her temper rise.

This…this…*gaggle* of men was no different than Jack. She was a person, not a sex object. She was a businesswoman, and existed for more than their viewing pleasure. How would they feel if she did the same thing to them?

She wasn't a toy or a blow-up doll. And she damn sure wasn't a reject who couldn't hold her man's attention. Dev, for all his faults, had helped her to see that. He'd helped her find her confidence again.

With a cool smile, she walked past them to the reception desk, where two dozen blood-red roses peered carnally out of a clear glass vase. Dev's apology?

"Ooh, Kylie, aren't they beautiful?" April said, clear envy in her voice.

They were. They were stunning. No doubt about it. But Kylie wished the group of men didn't have to witness her getting flowers at work. Kylie found the card and slipped it out of the plastic holder. She opened the envelope.

Can't wait to see you on Friday, babe. We have so much
to talk about.
Xoxo, Jack.

Her heart dropped into her Stuart Weitzman pumps. The roses were from Jack? And what did he think they had to talk about?

She took a step back from the reception desk, and then another.

"You must have made some guy very happy over the weekend, Miss Kent," called one of the investment bankers. "Your tailbone must be back in good working order."

Even April blinked in shock at the snarky, sexist comment.

As for Kylie, her jaw dropped. Had the bastard really said that? Really? Her spine stiffened as rage shot up it in a fireball.

"Kenny, you're so bad," another one of them said, snickering.

She didn't care that Milty was standing right there. She didn't care if the chairman of the federal reserve board or God himself was standing there—she wasn't going to let the rat bastard get away with this.

She turned and faced them all. "Actually, Kenny, the flowers aren't for me. They're for you, from the two hookers you hired to entertain you on Saturday. They send their condolences that the Viagra didn't help."

Kylie turned and walked away, without a single hitch in her stride. Behind her a thunderous silence ensued, followed by the sound of one man clapping. She didn't know who, until Milty's voice carried after her, ricocheting between the granite walls that housed the elevators.

"Boys," he said, "that is why Miss Kent is our new assistant vice president of small business loans. She's absolutely unflappable." He left off the last line, but it was clear to everyone present: *even in the face of morons like you, Kenny.*

Kylie stopped at the elevators and leaned weakly against the wall. She'd gotten a promotion? When? How?

Footsteps, measured, authoritarian, approached. She looked up to see Goldman standing there, a smile on his face.

"Mr. Goldman?"

"Call me Milty," he said.

"What, uh—"

"Priscilla Prentiss isn't returning to work," he said. "She's going to stay home with her children. And she highly recommended you for the job. I concur. So. We'll make it official to-morrow. I thought you might like to know, though." He stuck out his hand.

Dazed, Kylie shook it. "Thank you. I guess I fully expected to be fired after what I said to Kenny."

Milty laughed. "Not at all. He was way out of line. And you showed that you're capable of handling yourself beauti-fully with the big boys. I don't want someone who falls apart over that kind of thing. I want someone who can take off the gloves and fight back. Anyway. Tomorrow we'll talk about your responsibilities and compensation. See you then."

Kylie tried to take it in. She was actually sorry that Pris-cilla wasn't coming back, but glad of the opportunity. She felt half-exultant...and half-empty. She'd achieved her big short-term goal, which meant she was on the right career track.

She wanted to share the news with someone. She wanted to share the news, in fact, with Dev. But especially in the face of his performance Saturday night and this new promotion at the bank, she needed to cut ties with him.

Devon McKee represented a conflict of interest, a danger to her career. Not to mention that he'd be bad for her image as an executive. She pictured him showing up at a corporate function in those black leather pants of his.

Jack, on the other hand...

27

JACK PICKED UP KYLIE at seven o'clock on Friday. She'd had her hair washed and blown out at her salon and she wore a beautiful white silk halter blouse with a tropical print on it, with an over-the-knee white skirt and high heels.

She knew she looked her best, but Jack's admiring gaze didn't make her feel nearly as good as she'd imagined.

Potsy had the bad taste to come out, wind his way around Jack's ankles and purr. So much for animal instinct.

Actually, she couldn't fault Potsy for liking Jack, since they'd lived in the same condo for over a year, and that whole feeding issue was bound to confuse him where her ex was concerned. There was just something about the guy who fed him canned tuna and bagged kibble.

Potsy's standards were low, but he didn't know any better.

"Ready?" asked Jack, giving the cat a peremptory scratch on the head and brushing cat fur off his pant legs. He looked at his watch. "We have reservations at seven-thirty."

"Yes!" Kylie said, with a bright, fake smile. Why had she agreed to this? It was too weird.

Her ex looked as though he'd stepped off the cover of *GQ*, in another pair of his immaculately pressed khaki pants and a blue dress shirt. He wore woven-leather loafers with tassels on them and a matching woven leather belt. They were the same light caramel color as his hair, and she wondered if that was by design.

As he turned, she saw the corner of his wallet, and it, too, was caramel leather. So was the accent on his key-chain. And the seats in his dark blue BMW sedan, which was bigger and newer than the one he'd driven while they were engaged, but otherwise looked exactly the same.

Kylie complimented him on the car, because he seemed to expect it. He dropped the information that he'd gone to the competition, a rival medical supply company, for a big raise and promotion.

"It's a lot more headaches and responsibility, though," he added.

"How did you—" Kylie broke off. It wasn't very nice to ask him how he'd gone from fired, porn-and-pill-addicted bum to a big job with a competitor.

But Jack wasn't stupid. "How did I make the jump? Connections. My dad went to business school with a guy on the board. And we finessed some things on my résumé."

Finessed. In other words, he'd lied. And because of the *connections,* nobody had checked up on him. The world was easier for some people than it was for others, that was for sure.

She sat back in the buttery leather seat and thought about how she'd beat up on Dev for lying about the goldfish. But to his credit, Dev had been brutally honest about everything else in his life, whether or not it reflected well on him.

She shook her head and sighed. Dev. If she didn't know better, and if she weren't still disgusted with him, she might think she missed the guy.

Jack steered his elegant, purring BMW through the madness that was downtown Miami, and she found herself contrasting it with Dev's flashy, rumbling, cayenne-red Corvette.

Jack didn't take any corners on two wheels. He didn't fly through yellow lights. He drove sedately, like an old man.

No insults or zingers crackled through the atmosphere. No unseemly, magnetic sexual tension kept her on edge. And there were no lascivious glances or promises from Jack to chew off her skirt.

Kylie realized to her horror that she was bored already, and they hadn't even gotten to the restaurant.

Speaking of restaurants, Jack was ferrying her to South Beach. He crossed the Julia Tuttle causeway, humming. Within minutes he turned down Collins and then took a right, swinging past the little parking lot a couple of blocks from Dev's bar, where she'd been leaving her car.

"Jack, where are we eating?" she asked, getting a bad feeling in the pit of her stomach.

"Well, since you had to work so hard waiting tables there last weekend, I made reservations at Bikini for tonight. Someone can wait on *you* for a change." Jack smiled at her as he pulled the car up to the valet guys and unfastened his seat belt.

Oh, no. No, no, no. This was all wrong. If she'd felt weird before, Kylie now felt completely off-kilter, as if the whole globe were about to roll backward and squish her underneath it.

But Jack didn't ask if she was happy with his choice of restaurant. He was already out of the car and waiting for her to join him after the valet handed her out.

How could she go on a date with another guy to Bikini? Dev would hate her. Unless she found him first and told him that this wasn't really a date. It was merely a courtesy.

"Jack, I really don't want to eat here. Can we go someplace else?"

"What are you talking about? Don't be silly, Kylie. This place is the hottest new thing. Do you know that Bikini is completely booked for the next three months?" Jack said.

That's so great for Dev.

"I had to pull some strings—call in a favor with a guy I know at American Express in order to get in. But here we are." He looked smug.

"Jack, I could have gotten us a table if you'd told me," she reminded him. "My bank did the business loan."

He shrugged. "I wanted to surprise you." He slid his hand under her hair and caressed the skin left bare by the halter. She shivered, but not with pleasure. Then he propelled her toward the door.

Bikini was hopping, even at the grossly unfashionable time of 7:30 p.m. Generally speaking, south Floridians kept Latin hours, often not dining until ten o'clock at night, and not hitting the clubs until well after that. But she and Jack were gringos.

An unfamiliar hostess greeted them and handed them off to a waiter she'd never seen before, either. Of course after last weekend, Dev would have had to hire almost all new ones.

The guy seated them and said he'd be right back to take their drink orders. Kylie searched the room for Dev, but didn't see him anywhere. Jack, oddly enough, excused himself from the table and headed for the back, leaving her sitting alone.

DEV WAS ACTUALLY SITTING in his office inputting receipts into the Excel file Kylie had set up when he overheard a guy asking one of his waiters to drop an engagement ring into a glass of champagne for his girlfriend. Even as a cynic, Dev had to admit it was a romantic gesture. He went to the door.

A guy with light brown, sort of blondish hair pulled a ring out of the pocket of his khaki pants and held it out toward Bucky, who eyed it, clearly awed. The stone was at least two carats.

"You want me to take it out to her?" Dev asked, wondering vaguely why the man looked familiar. "I'm the owner."

"Oh, hey. That would be great, man. I really appreciate it."

"What table?" Dev asked Bucky.

"Fourteen."

"Okay. You run get the glasses, kid, and I'll get a bottle of—what, Dom? Taittinger? Perrier-Jouet?"

"Dom," said the guy.

"I'm Dev, by the way. Devon McKee." He stuck out his hand.

"John Hayward. People call me Jack." They shook hands.

"Good to meet you, Jack." Dev ignored the instant spasm of dislike he felt for the guy. His name wasn't his fault, after all. He walked into the kitchen and retrieved a bottle of Dom Pérignon from the refrigerator, pushing aside renegade memories of Kylie.

He'd wondered all week whether he should call her. But mortification was a powerful demotivator. Maybe he'd be over it in a few more days. Maybe not.

He waved at the crazed Bodvar—who'd had the nerve to hit him up for a raise on Monday—and returned to where Hayward waited with his ring. He'd uncorked the bubbly by the time Bucky showed up with the champagne flutes, and they got it all set up.

Hayward preceded him into the dining room. Dev gave him a couple of minutes to get seated again, and then headed around the curved partition and toward table fourteen.

The woman sitting there with her back to him had blond hair just like Kylie's. She had smooth, tanned shoulders like Kylie's, too. Dev almost stumbled right through table nine as he came to the awful, catastrophic conclusion that the woman *was* Kylie.

He stood stock-still with the glasses in his hand, focused on the back of her head, and then her profile as she turned to see what her date was staring at.

"Dev?" she said, and had the nerve to look happy to see

him. While she had a cozy reunion with the Jack-ass in *his* restaurant. "Hey, I was looking for you but you must have been in back."

He still stood there paralyzed, four feet away.

"Oh, you brought us champagne. How nice." She had the grace to look uncomfortable, at least, as her gaze went from him to Jack and then back to him. "Um. Devon, this is Jack Hayward. Jack, Devon McKee."

Yeah. I offer you two dicks. He offers you two carats.

"We've met," Dev said, struggling to keep his tone even. He wanted to throw the flutes on the floor and stomp them and the ring into slivers.

Jack nodded and eyed Dev with clear meaning. "We're thirsty, McKee."

He really wasn't sure he could pick up his feet if he wanted to. They were rooted to the floor, rooted in absolute certainty that he could not allow this to happen. Kylie could not get re-engaged to this creep who matched his shoes to his hair. And especially not in Bikini, the restaurant that she'd helped Dev launch.

He wanted to throw up.

He wanted to dive across the table and rip out Jack's throat. Stomp on his face. Tear off his legs.

She couldn't.

She wouldn't.

Would she?

But this wasn't Dev's call to make. It was hers.

Dev swallowed hard. He tried to calm his thundering pulse and get his stomach to quit blocking his airway. He unstuck his left foot from the ground, then his right one. And he forced himself toward the table, carrying another guy's ring to the woman he loved.

He set the glasses down in front of Jack and Kylie. "Congratulations," he managed to say hoarsely. And then he turned and walked away.

28

"WHAT?" KYLIE SAID. "What do you mean?" Then she looked at her glass. There, nestled in the bottom of it, was something that sparkled.

"Oh, God."

Jack smiled smugly at her. Complacently. "It's two carats. Bigger than your other one. What d'you say, Kylie? Let's put this team back together again."

So that's what he'd meant when he'd said they had a lot to talk about. Except they didn't. This conversation was over before it even began.

"No," Kylie said, shaking her head.

The smile disappeared from Jack's face. "What's the matter?"

"Jack, you've completely misinterpreted this whole evening. I never—" She threw a desperate look over her shoulder at Dev, who moved toward the back of the restaurant like a man on his way to face a firing squad.

"Is it not big enough for you?" Jack asked. "We can trade it in for three carats if you want to, but—"

"You're missing the point. I'm sorry, but I don't want to marry you."

"Of course you do, now that I'm over that little episode." He laughed. "I've grown. I've changed."

"So have I." Kylie pushed back her chair. He might have kicked his pill-and-porn habit. He might have a great job. He might look more fit and healthy. But he was still the same guy: the one who was perfect for her on the surface, on paper, but deep down was all wrong.

And Dev, with his black leather pants and his gold chain and spiky hair…Dev, with his fish fables and his checkered past—he was all right.

"Jack," she said gently, "no offense, but you couldn't possibly change enough for me. This isn't going to work. It never really did." She got up, intent on hurrying to intercept Dev before he got so drunk that he thought he had *three* dicks.

But before she could move, Jack's hand shot out and gripped her painfully around the wrist. "Sit down," he ordered.

"What? No." She tried to pull away, but he wouldn't let go.

"People are looking. You're not going to humiliate me in public." Jack ground out the words. "Sit down, drink your champagne and put the ring on your finger. Just do it."

"I'm not your puppet, Jack. I didn't ask you to propose to me in a crowded restaurant—or anywhere else, for that matter. So get your hands off me." She tore loose from his grip but he caught her arm instead, digging his fingers in painfully.

"Sit. The. Hell. Down. Bitch."

She gasped in pain and shock. "Let go of me or I will scream."

"No, you won't. Because I'll make big trouble for you at your little bank. My father's a buddy of the CEO's. How do you think the board will react if we tell them that you've been blowing Milty Goldman in the parking lot on your lunch hour?"

"You wouldn't dare, you bastard."

"Is that right?" A nasty smile played around his lips. "Sit down, Kylie."

She told him to do something anatomically impossible.

"Is there a problem, here?" Dev's voice came from over her shoulder, calm and very cold.

"No. Why would there be a problem?" Jack asked, baring his teeth. He still didn't turn her loose.

"I suggest that you release the lady, asshole." Dev's voice had gone arctic.

"And I suggest that you mind your own damned business." Jack's fingers only tightened on her arm, and she winced as the pain quotient went up.

That was when Dev's fist plowed into Jack's face, knocking him backward out of his chair.

Dev then upended her champagne glass into Jack's plate, grabbed the ring and wadded it into a napkin. As Jack struggled to get up, Dev jumped on him and shoved the napkin into his mouth.

"Get out!" he said. "And take your lousy ring with you."

Two men at neighboring tables had surged forward to pull Dev off of Jack if necessary, but he'd made his point and he was done. He got up and turned to Kylie while the men helped Jack to his feet.

"Are you all right?" Dev's face was white, his jaw set.

She nodded, speechless—because in that instant, she fully realized it: she was in love with him. Hopelessly in love. Then she threw herself into his arms and kissed him.

"HAVE I EVER TOLD YOU that you have a peculiar, repulsive appeal?" Kylie murmured later as they shivered naked in the walk-in fridge.

"You may have mentioned it," Dev said, before taking one of her breasts into his mouth.

"Mmm. Oh…"

"Mmm?" Dev inquired.

"Yes. In fact, I think you might just do," Kylie said.

"Do? Do what, exactly?"

"Me."

"I'll do you, honey." Dev picked her up and slid into her to the hilt. "I'll do you 'til you beg me to stop."

"Never," she said, hooking her ankles around his waist.

"You never want me to stop?"

"Nope."

"Sounds good to me."

Someone pounded on the heavy insulated door. "Hey! We need produce out of there. And cream for the lobster bisque. Can you hurry it up?"

Dev sighed. "I guess leaving a Do Not Disturb sign on the door was a bad idea."

"We're already very disturbed," Kylie said. "But I love you beyond reason."

"I love you, too." He kissed her, as the pounding on the door commenced again. "Do you still think I should date a whole bunch of other women, like you ordered me to?"

"No. Changed my mind about that."

"Oh, okay. Just checking. So…you want to move in with me? Get a plant together? Maybe another fish?"

She laughed. "As long as you never drink liquor again."

Dev pulled back and looked into her eyes. "You have my solemn oath. Never."

Kylie nodded. She believed him.

"So is that a yes?" Dev persisted. "You'll move in?"

She broke into a smile. "That's a yes."

He kissed her. And kissed her. "That's the best news I've had in a decade." And he kissed her some more.

She finally pulled away, breathless. "We can get a third fish. But Potsy gets to pick him out."

"Potsy," Dev said, without enthusiasm. "I forgot about him."

"You'll grow to love him as much as you love me."

"Uh huh. Right."

"Hey, Dev?"

"What?"

"Have I ever told you that your two dicks make up for your personality?"

"I'm so glad to hear that. I really am..."

* * * * *

PASSION

Harlequin® *Blaze*

COMING NEXT MONTH
AVAILABLE MARCH 27, 2012

#675 BLAZING BEDTIME STORIES, VOLUME VI
Bedtime Stories
Tori Carrington and Kate Hoffmann

#676 JUST ONE KISS
Friends with Benefits
Isabel Sharpe

#677 WANT ME
It's Trading Men!
Jo Leigh

#678 ONE MAN RUSH
Double Overtime
Joanne Rock

#679 NIGHT AFTER NIGHT...
Forbidden Fantasies
Kathy Lyons

#680 RUB IT IN
Island Nights
Kira Sinclair

HBCNM0312

REQUEST YOUR FREE BOOKS!
2 FREE NOVELS PLUS 2 FREE GIFTS!

Harlequin® Blaze™

red-hot reads!

YES! Please send me 2 FREE Harlequin® Blaze™ novels and my 2 FREE gifts (gifts are worth about $10). After receiving them, if I don't wish to receive any more books, I can return the shipping statement marked "cancel." If I don't cancel, I will receive 6 brand-new novels every month and be billed just $4.49 per book in the U.S. or $4.96 per book in Canada. That's a saving of at least 14% off the cover price. It's quite a bargain. Shipping and handling is just 50¢ per book in the U.S. and 75¢ per book in Canada.* I understand that accepting the 2 free books and gifts places me under no obligation to buy anything. I can always return a shipment and cancel at any time. Even if I never buy another book, the two free books and gifts are mine to keep forever.

151/351 HDN FEQE

Name	(PLEASE PRINT)

Address	Apt. #

City	State/Prov.	Zip/Postal Code

Signature (if under 18, a parent or guardian must sign)

Mail to the **Reader Service:**
IN U.S.A.: P.O. Box 1867, Buffalo, NY 14240-1867
IN CANADA: P.O. Box 609, Fort Erie, Ontario L2A 5X3

Not valid for current subscribers to Harlequin Blaze books.

Want to try two free books from another line?
Call 1-800-873-8635 or visit www.ReaderService.com.

* Terms and prices subject to change without notice. Prices do not include applicable taxes. Sales tax applicable in N.Y. Canadian residents will be charged applicable taxes. Offer not valid in Quebec. This offer is limited to one order per household. All orders subject to credit approval. Credit or debit balances in a customer's account(s) may be offset by any other outstanding balance owed by or to the customer. Please allow 4 to 6 weeks for delivery. Offer available while quantities last.

Your Privacy—The Reader Service is committed to protecting your privacy. Our Privacy Policy is available online at www.ReaderService.com or upon request from the Reader Service.

We make a portion of our mailing list available to reputable third parties that offer products we believe may interest you. If you prefer that we not exchange your name with third parties, or if you wish to clarify or modify your communication preferences, please visit us at www.ReaderService.com/consumerschoice or write to us at Reader Service Preference Service, P.O. Box 9062, Buffalo, NY 14269. Include your complete name and address.

HB11B

Harlequin® Blaze™

red-hot reads

**Sizzling fairy tales
to make every fantasy come true!**

Fan-favorite authors
Tori Carrington and Kate Hoffmann
bring readers

Blazing Bedtime Stories, Volume VI

MAID FOR HIM...

Successful businessman Kieran Morrison doesn't dare hope for
a big catch when he goes fishing. But when he wakes up one
night to find a beautiful woman seemingly unconscious on the
deck of his sailboat, he lands one bigger than he could ever
have imagined by way of mermaid Daphne Moore.
But is she real? Or just a fantasy?

OFF THE BEATEN PATH

Greta Adler and Alex Hansen have been friends for seven years.
So when Greta agrees to accompany Alex at a mountain retreat
owned by a client, she doesn't realize that Alex has a different
path he wants their relationshiop to take.
But will Greta follow his lead?

Available April 2012 wherever books are sold.

*Taft Bowman knew he'd ruined any chance he'd had
for happiness with Laura Pendleton when he drove her
away years ago...and into the arms of another man,
thousands of miles away. Now she was back, a widow
with two small children...and despite himself, he was
starting to believe in second chances.*

*Harlequin Special® Edition® presents a new installment
in USA TODAY bestselling author
RaeAnne Thayne's miniseries,
THE COWBOYS OF COLD CREEK.*

*Enjoy a sneak peek of
A COLD CREEK REUNION*

Available April 2012 from Harlequin® Special Edition®

A younger woman stood there, and from this distance he
had only a strange impression, as though she was somehow standing on an island of calm amid the chaos of the
scene, the flashing lights of the emergency vehicles, shouts
between his crew members, the excited buzz of the crowd.

And then the woman turned and he just about tripped
over a snaking fire hose somebody shouldn't have left
there.

Laura.

He froze, and for the first time in fifteen years as a fire-
fighter, he forgot about the incident, his mission, just what
the hell he was doing here.

Laura.

Ten years. He hadn't seen her in all that time, since
the week before their wedding when she had given him
back his ring and left town. Not just town. She had left the
whole damn country, as if she couldn't run far enough to

get away from him.

Some part of him desperately wanted to think he had made some kind of mistake. It couldn't be her. That was just some other slender woman with a long sweep of honey-blond hair and big, blue, unforgettable eyes. But no. It was definitely Laura. Sweet and lovely.

Not his.

He was going to have to go over there and talk to her. He didn't want to. He wanted to stand there and pretend he hadn't seen her. But he was the fire chief. He couldn't hide out just because he had a painful history with the daughter of the property owner.

Sometimes he hated his job.

Will Taft and Laura be able to make the years recede...or is the gulf between them too broad to ever cross?

Find out in
A COLD CREEK REUNION
Available April 2012 from Harlequin® Special Edition®
wherever books are sold.

Celebrate the 30th anniversary
of Harlequin® Special Edition® with a bonus story
included in each Special Edition® book in April!

HSEEXP0412